I ZOMBIE

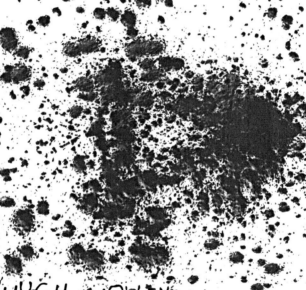

BY HUGH HOWEY

I ZoMBiE

Copyright © 2012 by Hugh Howey

Cover design by Mike Tabor
Edited by David Gatewood and Gay Murrill
Interior design and layout by Hugh Howey
Photography by Hugh Howey and Amber Lyda

ISBN-13: 978-1477401293
ISBN-10: 1-47740129-6

www.hughhowey.com

Give feedback on the book at:
hughhowey@gmail.com
Twitter: @hughhowey

Printed in the U.S.A

ABANDON HOPE...

...AND BASH IN HER SKULL BEFORE YOU GO.

Part I ✦ The Hunger

Gloria • Michael Lane • Jennifer Shaw

1 ❖ Gloria

There was a hole in Gloria's smile the size of an apple. When she ate, much of what she chewed passed through her cheek and spilled down her neck. And when a scent caught her attention—usually the smell of the living— she would lift her head to take a sniff and feel the air pass through her open face to hammer her rotting teeth.

Gloria was dead, and so were her teeth, but they were all still painfully sensitive to the exposure.

Bowing her head back over her meal, she tried not to watch what she was doing. The stench and texture were visceral enough, the taste both revolting and sickly soothing. A pack of five or so ripped into the man, the scene calmer than a big feed. There were grunts and contented smacking sounds, not the angry roars from those on the outside clawing to get in. Instead, she and four other monsters huddled together like hyenas on the Serengeti. They rubbed shoulders and listened to the sounds of flesh tearing and tendons snapping, the hotness of the man up to her elbows, blood dripping from her chin.

Gloria ate, and much of what she chewed spilled down her neck.

The revulsion she felt was mental. Gloria *wished* it were physical. She wanted to vomit, dearly wanted to vomit, but she couldn't. The meat of the man tasted too good. It satisfied too deep and strong a craving, this new hunger that reminded her of all her old and equally primal urges.

There were two years in high school when Gloria had tried to become a vegetarian. This monster she had turned into reminded her of those years, of the meals that came after she'd given up trying to be good. She remembered how badly she had felt for that chicken even as she tore through its meat. There was a night out with friends, laughing, spilling beer, a hundred screens of sports she cared nothing about, and baskets of wings. She had held one, fingers sticky with sauce, a bite taken out of the flesh, and she had looked down, had seen those tendons and bone, and had realized what she was doing.

Even then, Gloria had known it was wrong. But she loved it too much. The taste was always stronger than her compassion. And so she ate and felt sick at the same time. She loved the meat and hated herself.

The dead body in the blue jeans and ruined button-up reminded her of that chicken wing. It was barely recognizable as a person anymore, covered in its own sauce. The pack grew to seven, and the man's lower half was dragged away and fought over. More yummy disgustingness spilled out from his torso and spread across the warm pavement. The monster across from Gloria scrambled for the same slick ropes as she. The purple meat slid through both of their hands, their lips dribbling sauce back down on their food, fighting for scraps.

This other monster's fingers were missing from one of his hands, bitten off, leaving him with a stump. Gloria saw the familiar black char of an original wound, the bite that had infected this man, working its way up his wrist. Still, he clawed for the meat with what was left of his hand. Like Gloria, he was only half in control of what he was doing. They were along for the ride, each of them. At the wheel— but without the power steering.

2 ✦ Michael Lane

Michael remembered being a boy. He remembered the times from before. Michael could remember *everything*.

He remembered doctors in white coats telling him that his mother was still in there, that she was still alive behind those glassy eyes and that distant stare. In his more hopeful moments he would sit by her side, hold her hand, and believe them. He would pretend it was true.

And when her wheelchair squeaked and rattled with another shaking fit, Michael would squeeze her withered and trembling hands and talk to her, try to reason with her, ask her to please stop.

These were the times when he believed the doctors, when he thought his mother was still in there, peering out. He would talk to her like this when he was most hopeful. He would talk to her calmly.

And then there were days when he didn't believe, when he couldn't believe—and he would have to scream.

Michael Lane remembered screaming at his mother. He remembered this as he staggered through the apartment, knocking over furniture, chasing her hissing cat.

"Wake up!" he would yell at his mom, back when he could yell at anything.

"Wake the fuck up!"

And he would shake her. He would want to hit her, but he never did. At least, he didn't think so.

It had been tempting at times. Not because he thought it would do her any good or snap her out of the degenerative palsy into which she had fallen, but because punching a hole in the wall didn't make him feel any better. He wasn't pissed off at the wall. Walls were supposed to just sit there. That's what walls did.

His mother's old black cat stood in the corner by the radiator, its spine arched, fur spiked, pink tongue and white teeth visible as it hissed at him. The damn thing was thin as a shadow. Starving. Michael was starving, too. He closed in, remembering the doubts he'd had about his mother's condition. Those doubts had nagged at him for years.

What if his mother was just acting? What if this was her way of avoiding the world? He hadn't been able to stop thinking these things. Michael had watched his father crawl inside a bottle and die there just so he didn't have to get up and go to work. It wasn't long before his mom retreated behind a vacant gaze, leaving him and his sister to pay the bills, to change her stinking bags, to roll her from one sunny patch by the window to another. His mother had become a potted plant they fretted over. No, that wasn't right. Couldn't plants at least turn their heads and follow the sun? Weren't they better than her in that way?

Falling forward as much as lunging, Michael seized the weak and cornered cat. Sharp claws gouged his hands, burning where they broke the skin. He ignored this—he had no choice—and concentrated on the past. The times he had screamed at his mother were painful memories, so Michael orbited those. Pain was a distraction from what he knew he was about to do. And so he tried to remember if he had ever hit his mother, even a little. He couldn't. Couldn't remember. Maybe he had.

The cat clawed at his face as he bowed his head into its fur. It batted at his unblinking eyes, and Michael—the memory of Michael—recoiled in fear. But the body he was trapped inside did not pull back. The hunger was too great, that mad craving for meat too strong. Not this meat, perhaps. Not cat meat. But he was barricaded inside his apartment with little else. He had locked himself inside, thinking he was safe, that he'd be okay. But he wasn't. He wasn't safe. He wasn't okay.

Michael's teeth sank past the fur to tear at the animal's flesh. The cat was a screaming, writhing blur. It clawed at his open eyes, tore at his ears, while Michael ate.

He couldn't stop himself.

This was not him.

The blood ran down his throat, warm and foul, the cat's shrieks fading to rattling groans, and he could taste it. He could taste the meat. But this was not him. This was not Michael Lane.

Michael remembered being a boy, once.

He remembered the doctors telling him things, how a person could be locked away inside a body they couldn't control.

And Michael never believed them, not really.

Until now.

3 ❖ Jennifer Shaw

A grist of bees. A bevy of deer. A mob of—
What was a mob again? Yaks?

Emus. It was emus, Jennifer decided. But what animal made up a gang? Or a boil? Wasn't there some creature that combined to form a bloat? Bloat was taken, she was pretty sure.

Jennifer drifted back to the games her father played. This was but one of many. She remembered hanging from his arm, her sister on the other side, as he swung them through Central Park Zoo. He called them monkeys—

"A band!" she and her sister would squeal.

"You little gorillas."

"A troop!"

"You smelly baboons."

"A flange!"

"I'm not smelly," her sister would add, pouting.

Up and down the tree of life they would climb, learning useless facts that made their peers roll their eyes and their teachers clap with delight. Their father never taught them state capitals or anything normal. Nothing other people might already know. He filled their heads with reptiles and minerals and trivia. Jennifer never saw a garter snake slither through the grass without thinking: *There goes Massachusetts.*

"A family is more than just its members," their father had said. "Together, we become something *different.*"

He said this a lot after their mother left. Swinging them through the zoo, he had shown his girls all the animals that hate to be alone, that prefer to go in groups. Each group had its own name, he taught them. In company they were something more than they could be in solitude.

So what was this, Jennifer wondered? What had she become? What was she a part of?

It couldn't be a *plague*; those were locusts. Couldn't be an *intrusion* because of the roach. And wasn't a group of midges called a *bite?* She was pretty sure that was right. Shame, that one. And mosquitoes were a *scourge.* All the good ones were taken.

Herd. Herd was overdone, as was pack. Too many animals shared those. Too obvious.

And then it came to her.

It came to her as the skull Jennifer had become trapped inside lolled down, as the nose that used to be hers twitched at the smell of meat.

An arm lay on the pavement, a torn sleeve wrapping it like a cloak, a cloud of flies drawn to the rotting meat. Its owner was long gone.

Jennifer had no appetite for it. She lumbered onward, no longer in control, forced to see whatever her head saw as it followed some scent, some impulse, some new reflex.

And for a moment—because of the dismembered arm, perhaps—the direction of her gaze allowed Jennifer to study the feet, *her* feet, and the feet of those around her. The bare feet and the feet in ragged slippers; the work boots and the worn trainers; the feet sliding and dragging; the feet of the people bumping into her, all of them moving in one direction, *upwind*, toward the smell of living meat.

She was one of them, and Jennifer knew what she was, what the group would be called.

She filed this trivia away. She took it with her as she disappeared into the recesses of her recollections, back to the times before she joined this trembling mass, this vile and grotesque thing her flesh had become. She skipped into the past, swinging on her father's strong arms, beating her sister to calling this one out:

"A *shuffle*," she cried. "A shuffle of zombies!"

And the animals of Central Park Zoo paced inside their cages, watching her and her dead family stagger by.

And they were all afraid.

4 ❖ Michael Lane

Michael was suffering from withdrawal. He wasn't sure at first—it was hard to discern one madness from the other—but now he knew.

He still had the taste of cat blood in his mouth, could feel this voice in his head, this lunatic starving for meat, this new animal in control of his body. And behind the thick curtain of horror that had drawn shut across his awareness, a tiny, familiar, persistent shout could be heard: he needed a fix. His veins hungered for the prick of steel, for the warm flow of numbness and that perfect release. He needed it now more than ever before. An overdose, Michael decided, would be fucking heavenly. A way to go. Any way to go for good.

The kit was on top of the fridge. Everything was there to help him die in bliss. He could sate the urge to which he'd been a slave for longer than he could remember, for longer than he'd ever been in control of himself, for almost as long as his mother had been seized by her blank stares and her shivering fits.

But now there was a new monster guiding his hand, dictating the direction of his mindless stagger. And this new thirst, this awful craving, carried him not toward the kitchen, but toward the door to his mother's room.

The cat was dead. Michael had eaten most of it. Its fur was still stuck in his throat, his body too dumb to cough it up. It left a powerful tickle he could do nothing about.

With the animal gone, there was only one other scent of flesh nearby, only one other piece of meat in the tiny apartment.

Michael's bloodstained hands banged and gouged at the door, swimming toward the smell of flesh on the other side. He cried out in silent despair, knowing what the monster in him craved. There was no controlling it. He couldn't even command his swollen tongue to lie still—it lolled with every grunt and seemed to fill his mouth with its writhing. It felt liable to choke him.

His fingernails caught on the door's panels and bent backward. The smears of cat blood on the door looked like something a child would come home from school with and be proud of, or something one of the museums uptown would charge millions for. Michael felt a swallowed laugh, thinking of that door hanging on a wall with his name under it. The world's first zombie art. His laugh came out a gurgle.

The gory brush strokes, meanwhile, worked their way toward the doorknob. Had he been thinking about how to open the door? He tried not to, tried to conceal this knowledge from his terrible side, but picturing the mechanism brought it to the surface. One monster spoke to another, and crimson claws fell to the fake brass.

Michael couldn't control it, couldn't stop himself. All he could do was spill secrets to this dark animal inside him. All he could do—as ever—was betray his mother. Or maybe it wasn't him. Maybe it was chance, he thought, as he watched a torturous eternity of banging and fumbling. Maybe it was just bad luck, all out of his control.

The handle twisted, and the door popped open. Michael lurched forward, a passenger, a man beating on a window, begging the conductor to stop, to let him out, to let him just jump out and please run him the fuck over.

His mother was by the window, right where he'd left her two days earlier. The curtains rustled in the breeze. It was cold in the room, and the smell of flesh was intoxicating. It bled into his rush for a fix. It confused him, this lust for eating the living. A warm patch grew around his crotch, and Michael realized his bladder was letting loose. He was an animal. Untrained. Barbaric. Just needs and impulses, cravings, and a mass of muscles that drove him toward sating those cravings. Simple as that. His ability to do as he chose—if ever he'd possessed that skill at all—was gone.

Michael staggered toward the open window and sobbed inwardly for his mother. The new hunger inside him swelled and grew until it drowned out even the urge for a fix. Even that.

His hands were still sticky from the cat, still matted with fur, his stomach lurching around the foulness he'd consumed, the ropes of guts, the sinew and muscle, the dark pouch that had slid down his throat, the purple sacs, all the shit he'd been able to name long enough to pass a goddamned biology test years ago, now just one revolting taste after another.

All this was on his breath and in his mind as Michael fell upon his still and defenseless mother.

Withdrawing in horror, curling up in his former skull, tucking his imaginary knees against his chest, he tried his damnedest not to watch. He tried his damnedest not to taste. But teeth and tongue fell into soft flesh, and his mother didn't stir, didn't move a muscle. She just sat there, warm and still alive, the bag hanging from her chair overfull, wasting away in body, even though he knew—with horror he fucking knew—that she was still in there.

She was in there and trapped, suffering with him.

She had known.

She had known when he'd hit her, when he had slapped her face in frustration. Fuck, it was years ago. Years ago, but he'd done it. And all those times he'd shouted at her, shook her shoulders, told her to wake the fuck up ... she had known. Every time he had aimed her chair at the window before crawling out to smoke a joint, she had watched. She'd been forced to witness while he shot up on the sill, had been forced to sit there, unblinking, every time he collapsed in her old bed, gloriously high, the room reeking of her piss and shit.

Fuck.

Michael Lane had devoured his mother's soul in a feast of years, had done it while she sat, paralyzed, made to endure. He'd done that, a morsel at a time, not knowing he was doing it at all.

And now her body faintly rocked, her wide eyes and expressionless face lolling as he consumed the rest of her, as Michael's mad cravings ripped his mother's shell apart to get at what little inside still remained.

5 ❖ Gloria

Every day undead brought new discoveries, new horrors to learn and accept. It was how prison must've felt for Carl, Gloria decided. She could only imagine. Her husband would never talk about it, would never allow her to visit, and so she spent her lonely nights imagining. Picturing what he was going through. She decided it was a lot like this.

First fears were naïve, fears of never seeing family again, agony over luxuries lost, thinking of the places you couldn't go, things you couldn't eat, walls you couldn't climb. But more basic freedoms soon drown these out. There's the unnatural horror of not being able to walk in a straight line, of not being able to get out of a tight cell—

Jail cell. Human cell. Gloria felt like an embryo trapped in a womb. She saw what her brain saw, but her thinking was removed from the action. She was strapped to a bunk, inmates all around her, new horrors to learn at every turn.

Prison must be like this, she thought. First, you concern yourself with freedoms lost. But soon, new worries take precedence. She had gone from fearing for her safety to fearing for others. From the horror of being bitten to the horror of eating others. There was the pain of hunger—but the agony of a feed, of seeing what she did to others, was far worse.

She imagined what Carl had gone through those first days locked away. She had always thought he'd be missing her, couldn't understand why he didn't take her calls, allow her to visit, even write back. It was because he'd had other things to fear. Maybe something as simple as taking a shower. Or the daily badgering from some sadistic guard or inmate. Gloria didn't have to imagine any longer how a person might have to learn to become worse just to fit in— she knew. She knew what it was like to become something worse, all the while wondering if everyone around her was doing the same, being something they weren't.

This was just like prison, she decided. This was her solitary confinement, her mute holding cell, walls of her own flesh tailored as tightly as humanly possible.

What she wouldn't give for one good scream, for one glorious wail, one bone-trembling blast from cold and terrified lungs. But even this was a freedom snatched away from her—the most basic of freedoms gone. She couldn't even complain. Couldn't shout. The gurgles and groans that dribbled out, leaked from the hole in her smile, were the best that she could manage. It was all any of them could manage. Around her, stumbling through the streets, there was this chorus of stifled screams—a hellish and chilling choir. It was just one more horror to learn about her new life in prison, one more fact to get used to and to accept.

Gloria listened to the sounds she made, and her thoughts strayed from Carl and drifted to her grandfather. She could hear in her own rattling exhalations his dying voice. She could hear his groans and gurgles from that miserable and drawn-out death of his.

It had started small, with him forgetting things. And just as the family learned to cope with his blank stares and his groping for the right word, they had to worry about him wandering off. And as they got used to penning him up like a rooster, he started falling, banging his head on furniture, breaking his wrist. The bleeding in his brain from the fall in the driveway didn't help. Not enough. As bad as that day was for the family, it was only the beginning. Years later, Gloria would look back on those early struggles and wish he'd struck his head harder. She would wish that he didn't have to live and see what he would eventually become.

This was easier to admit now that she was beyond death herself, now that she was whatever she had turned into, now that she could wish a similar fate on herself. All these discoveries felt much the same, this coping with a new reality that gradually got worse and worse. It was a lot like prison, she imagined. A lot like hospital beds. A lot like life, in many ways. Youthful vigor becomes more rot than wisdom. Hopeful optimism is battered by harsh reality. Health and understanding seem to intersect in one's forties, the one peaking as the other begins its slow ascent.

Maybe you'll know one day what you should've taken the time to appreciate. Maybe it'll be when your knees start popping, when your hands no longer work like they should. It probably won't be any sooner.

Gloria began to appreciate all she once had somewhere between 2nd Avenue and 3rd. It was a week ago, during her first feed, while tasting human flesh. Burying her head in some dead man's abdomen, she'd had this spark of awareness that all the bullshit fears of her former life were nothing. Worries over money, over Carl, her grandmother, over not having kids of her own, never once thinking how amazing it was to breathe and not feel the cool air flowing through one's cheek and hammering sensitive teeth, never once going outside to walk in whatever direction she chose, just because she could.

There were things she could now admit. Like wanting her grandfather dead because it affected her routine, because it meant guilt-ridden visits to that nasty hospital. She never gave much thought to him being inside there, terrified, dizzy, all alone. Not until somewhere between 2nd Avenue and 3rd when she'd felt it, too. Not until this sudden awakening that *here* was her eternity, eating those who themselves were starving, shuffling after gaunt survivors as they sprinted terrified through the streets, often alone, hoping to find sanctuary or company, armed with guns or sticks or nothing at all.

This was her life, roaming the city day and night while these startled fish flapped through shallowing streams, while the living ran out of water, while they swam from the sharks and tumbled into nets.

Gloria remembered her first feed, that older man, and how her thoughts back then had also turned to her grandfather. There she was, killing a man, and wishing she wasn't. Wishing she could stop. The irony struck her there in the middle of that intersection, the years of keeping her grandfather alive, saving him over and over, and wishing she hadn't.

The shadows of Manhattan stretched across its wide streets. One of Gloria's shoes was gone; she didn't remember when or how. It'd probably happened at night. Here was another prison discovery, another thing to learn about life behind bars. It was the fitful, waking sleep. Never quite asleep, though. Always moving. Always standing or crawling. There was no stop to anything anymore. It was hell eternal. It was hospital beds and reruns and fucking remote controls always out of reach—

Gloria's stomach churned. The sleep wasn't the worst part. Oh, not even the worst part. That would be the bowel movements. The same had been true of her grandfather. It had come in stages. Innocently enough, at first. A nice man in blue work pants on his knees in the bathroom installing handles by the toilet. He had spoken of his own grandmother. He told Gloria about these new bathtubs with little doors for getting in and out. Made it safer. Said the seals on them leaked sometimes, but it was worth it. Finding a puddle on the tile was better than finding a loved one with a broken hip, right? He said this with a smile, wiping his forehead with his sleeve, tightening that last screw on the handle and insisting Gloria look into them. Gloria had said she would.

Her grandfather barely had time to test that handle. He moved to bedpans and sponges before she or her sister got the chance to look into those bathtubs with their leaky doors. It happened so fast, his downhill slide. It went on forever and seemed to happen so fast. One moment, a stranger is installing a handle by his toilet. The next moment, the strongest and ablest man she had ever known is found sleeping in his own shit.

So fast.

The old washing machine broke down during those weeks. They cycled through a few sets of bed sheets, trying to keep up. The next step had been bags and tubes, dignity restored with plastic contraptions, family members wrinkling their noses, even those whose diapers he had long ago changed. They couldn't stomach what he had once endured. Their mighty old grandfather was now mucking up their routines.

Gloria's stomach churned, returning her to the here and now. The bowel movements were the worst, something to dread. The undead, like the barely living, they had no dignity. They ate their fellow man. They shat like birds on the wing. The guts of others spilled from tattered dresses. Gloria saw it all day ahead of her: the stained pants and the rivers of gore streaming out the cuffs. She could feel it coming in her own body, the horror brewing, cramps in her bowels as though her intestines were tying themselves in knots. And then the evacuation, the indignity, the hotness down her legs, clothes crusted fast to chapped and undead skin, a bare foot slipping in it, no memory of where that shoe went.

It wasn't a touch they put in the movies, Gloria thought. It wasn't something you thought about while that nice man was tugging on a silver bar by the toilet, testing the bolts, cleaning up after a job well done, gathering his tools. *We can get through this*, you think to yourself. The whole family tells themselves this. They can get through it. This is before the washing machine breaks down. This is before your brother breaks down. This is when you think you can handle the pain because you fool yourself into thinking it'll be brief. This is when they're locking your husband away for a few short years, putting an innocent man behind bars, and you tell yourself you can handle him being gone for a little while. This is before he succumbs to whatever that hell is like, before he's innocent no more, when you're lying in bed at night no longer fearing that he's cheating on you with some harlot, but that he's done other, unspeakable, horrible things.

This is before the years stretch out into what feels like a forever. When sick men refuse to die. When innocent men find something to be guilty of. When years jumble together like water beading up on glass.

Gloria thought of the men in her life she had lost while another man passed through her guts. She shambled on, foul and reeking, a single day's horror stretching out like the wide avenue before her, no end in sight, no more fooling herself, no more thinking: *I can take this*.

6 ✦ Jennifer Shaw

New York had long been a city of hurry. Even the tourists couldn't relax when they came on vacation. Jennifer watched them fly from one must-see to another, packing in shows, walking until their feet and backs hurt, always terrified they'd miss one more sight. Few could simply sit in a park and feed the birds. And yet, that was all any of them did anymore. Tourists strewn throughout the parks, feeding the birds until their bones showed. Resting.

The only thing that came in a hurry anymore was the sunsets. The light dwindled to the west without warning, impossibly tall buildings catching the last of the rays, shadows creeping up their gaunt faces and stretched necks until the sky turned the color of blood and finally the deep black of death.

This was when the misery of the shuffle grew impossibly worse. Jennifer found she couldn't sleep, didn't even know what that would mean anymore. Her body roamed eternal, her mind trapped. Entire city blocks would go by like sleepy miles on a long drive. She would snap alert and wonder how she got there, have a brief moment of panic like waking to a dead limb, fighting to control some horribly numb part of herself, all to no avail. That surge of adrenaline would soon subside as chemicals both useless and impotent faded into her dead flesh. These responses were only good for rattling her poor nerves. They were old ghosts of her former self, shaking useless and haunting chains.

The air grew cool with the setting sun, and Jennifer remembered those interminable drives across Long Island to see her parents, pushing herself late into the night after a long day of work. With the radio blaring and the windows down, her thoughts would tune out while her body cruised on auto. Coming to miles later, she would glance in the rearview mirror and marvel at turns she'd steered around with absolutely no awareness of them.

The walks at night were like those drives. Every grueling and frigid night since that boy bit her arm was like a dozen of those long drives. From sundown to sunup, the fitful non-sleep of scents and sounds, an occasional feed, the sad company of the groaning and jostling shuffle.

The cold of looming winter made it even easier to drift in and out. The chill worked itself deep into her bones, attacking her skin where it was bare. An early encounter with a handful of survivors had shredded her shirt, leaving it hanging from her belt in bloody tatters. Her thin bra offered little comfort. At night, her nipples grew sore from staying hardened so long. It was as if some parts of her were still alive, but only the parts that could add to her suffering.

When she was most miserable—in the dead of night with her nipples aching—her thoughts turned to the boy who had bit her. And invariably from there, she thought of the young man she had days later bitten in turn. Like her, the young man she had attacked managed to get away. It felt like the thing to do when it was happening. You're threatened, hormones and chemicals serve their purpose, instilling you with fear, and so your body wants to yank loose and flee.

But now she wasn't so sure. Maybe it was like a dog's bite, where pulling just made it worse. She'd watched an older man's eyes go dim during a feed, once. Enough of him had been eaten that he didn't have time to turn. There wasn't enough to come back. Jennifer had seen the last of that man's life leave his body, had felt him go perfectly still, and was beginning to count men like him among the lucky.

There was a desperate need to shiver, but she couldn't. It was worse than an itch she couldn't reach, a crippling form of paralysis. The sunset came like a switch flicked, the temperature plummeting, and Jennifer imagined wrapping her arms around her body, tried to will her hands to adjust the remains of her shredded shirt—

Instead, she trudged along, frozen and freezing, unable to move and unable to stop.

There were others among the shuffle who had it even worse. She felt horrible for the half-naked members, for those who looked as though they'd been bitten in their sleep and had somehow startled awake and managed to get away. They walked barefoot through the streets of broken glass and left smears of foul-smelling blood behind them.

Sights like these gradually faded as darkness fell across the city streets, smothering them like a heavy blanket. There hadn't been power in the tall buildings for over a week, and with the moon in full wane, the nighttime became a mass of shifting dead beneath a glittering sprinkle of stars. Bodies bumped against Jennifer, some of them still sticky from a feed the shuffle had shared earlier that day. What had been revolting the first few nights was now something different. A knock against her neighbor was the only touch she knew. If it wasn't this, it was the frantic clawing from a woman dying on the sidewalk, eyes wide with fear, shrieks turning to gurgles as Jennifer devoured her from belly to neck. It was a small thing, these bumps in the night. Small, but then it was the *only*.

The shuffle moved through the pitch black streets by scent and by feel, groans escaping from the most miserable among them. Evidence of survivors became more apparent after dark. The living stirred in the tall buildings with the bob and weave of flashlights, or the orangish flicker of fires that burned where fires should never be. Jennifer remembered her days of surviving. She remembered the black ring of char on carpets and expensive hardwoods as folders full of projects that seemed so dire weeks ago were tossed on as fuel for warmth. There were others up there doing today what weeks ago she had done. How safe did they think they were? How secure? The attack could come at any time for them. She knew. From out of nowhere, *BAM!* And then the running, the metallic taste of fear and the hollow and cool rasp of desperate lungs, the danger around every corner, new allies split up and separated, friends becoming monsters, sitting in a stall in a men's restroom, heels tucked up on the seat, growing numb. Shivering, back when she could.

Jennifer sniffed the air and saw the glitter of a fire high up in the heavens. What was life like for the living up there? Had it changed? Were people still subsisting on vending machine scraps? Food running low? Fights breaking out as fear and hunger took hold? She remembered how lonely it had felt. Anyone she had cared about or known had been stripped away from her, gone. She was left surviving with strangers. Getting to know people the next cubicle down. But they hadn't been as alone as they'd imagined. The hallways and floors of sameness had gradually become infested with small shuffles. Jennifer remembered running. She remembered the boy who bit her. If she had known, she would have just laid down and waited for her own eyes to dim, for her soul to escape.

The lights from a helicopter drifted among the stars, faintly blinking. They had grown fewer in recent days. Jennifer had hoped they would become more abundant. She had imagined them bringing supplies back in the time when she'd known hope. She had dreamed of them coming to haul away the living. Someone had said they'd seen this happen the first day or two. But those were private helicopters or ones with television station numbers on the side. The hunter green and black helicopters had soon replaced these, and they now hovered warily and only at a distance. They did nothing. And gone were the days of hope.

Now, when Jennifer saw a helicopter, she didn't imagine it bringing supplies. She pictured instead a man inside with a long gun trained across her shuffle. *Shoot*, she would plead to this young soldier. *Do it.* It comforted her to imagine the warmth of a red dot on the center of her forehead. She would silently scream and wave imagined limbs while she prayed for the bullet—but it never came. The helicopters simply hovered and watched, and Jennifer imagined they had their reasons. Maybe the members of the shuffle were still considered citizens. Hadn't there been a controversy once? Some woman with a man's name who had captivated America? A woman mostly gone, obviously not able to do anything but suffer, and yet that's all they would allow her to do.

Terry, right? What finally happened to her? Jennifer couldn't remember. The story had gone on too long for her to care.

Maybe it would be the same for her and the shuffle. Maybe the soldiers had orders to observe, nothing more. Maybe the politicians were meeting in chambers somewhere and dithering. Maybe the rest of America was glued to its televisions, watching in amazement, the elderly covering their mouths in shock, the young calling their friends and making jokes, saying how cool this shit was, could you believe it?

The helicopter lights moved against stars impossibly far away. All the lights were far away and out of reach. Jennifer remembered what a boyfriend had once told her about the stars, how they could be long gone but still shining. They could have burned out a thousand years ago, and their light would just now be reaching Earth. Gone and yet still there. Dead and seen at the same time.

Trash rustled in the darkness and stirred against Jennifer's ankles. There was no one left to come and sweep it away. It flew out from busted windows when the wind gusted. It gathered against the stoops and in the gutters. There was the smell of a fire somewhere, the distant whisper of conspiring flames, and Jennifer wondered what the rest of the world was doing. Were they succumbing to the same disease as her shuffle? Or did they watch, glued to their televisions once again as her city burned, as it all came crumbling down into streets of staggering ruin? Was this nothing more than another story for gaping jaws and wide eyes? Or would the soldiers in those faraway helicopters and the politicians in their chambers find some way to shut it down, to turn it off, to do anything more for her than change the fucking channel—?

7 ❖ Michael Lane

Michael ate his mother until his stomach burst. He could feel it rupture, could feel the organ stretch to bloating as he ate and kept on eating—and then it popped. His insides seemed to rearrange themselves as hastily swallowed mouthfuls of her flesh sagged down inside his own guts. Small bits of sinew and fat remained stuck between his teeth like roast beef.

One craving had been sated. Michael thought again of the little black kit on top of the fridge, the spoon with its heat-warped patina, a plastic orange lighter low on fluid, a needle that had dipped into his arm a thousand times, depositing its nectar like a honeybee, leaving him there on the sofa, head lolling in rapture, his mother drooling on herself in the next room as she filled a clear bag with frothing yellow piss.

From the neck up, she still looked the same. She was just as dead to him, just as eerily alive. Eyes open, she stared at an empty patch of floor. Her jaw was slack, her lips parted, as if she might finally say something, might finally snap out of it and fucking say something.

Michael felt the strain of her flesh inside his belly. The cat and his mother felt heavy in his abdomen, taut from taking in too much. Greedy. Always greedy.

He moved away from her, numb and disgusted with himself. Her chest stood open. Blood dripped from Michael's face, and contented grunts came from somewhere. Before him, his mother's belly was a gory pit, her ribs like pink fingers, like two open hands cradling nothing. Michael imagined crawling inside those glistening palms. He felt himself shrinking down, time zipping backwards, until he could fit inside her belly, could pull the flaps of loose skin over him like a blanket and return to the womb in which he had gestated. Maybe he could be born again, not like those assholes at NA but *really* born again. He wouldn't be a monster this time. He'd be someone who takes care of his mother. Someone who takes better care of himself.

A scent from the streets wafted in and filled the decrepit apartment, nicotine-stained curtains flapping in the breeze. Michael turned, his nose following the smell of the living, his guts full of his mother's guts but already thinking of the next fix. One more bite, like that bee sinking its stinger into his arm, filling him with its nectar.

He stood and staggered toward the window. He craved a cigarette. Michael always craved a smoke after a meal. A clay pot on the sill used to hold flowers when his sister was still coming around, before she'd given up on the two of them. Now it was mounded with crushed butts, filters stained muddy brown with tar, trails of ash everywhere.

Knocking over the pot, he clumsily groped through the open window and fell head-first onto the landing. His shoulder slammed painfully into the steel grating, and his overfull belly sloshed sickeningly. Michael could taste the bile and blood come partway up his throat before sinking back down. Almost reflexively, he righted himself, arms waving for balance, grunts and groans that were not his leaking past bloody lips.

Here was Michael's sanctuary, high above the streets. Here was where he sat between soaring highs, filling himself with deep inhalations of smoke to choke down the numb lows. Here was where he suffered the broad and empty valleys between his life's feeble peaks, so few in number.

Years suddenly felt like mere days. The past had piled up without him noticing. Maybe it was from living the same day over and over: cashing government checks, never enough to properly care for her, way more than was needed to *improperly* care for her, making deals with the leftovers, getting high, drifting off through the roof and into the clouds while his mom sat quietly in the next room.

Years and years that felt like days. It was all the same day. The same craving every moment, the itching urge, the temporary relief, the guilt and self-loathing, burning cigarettes down to the butt on the fire escape, peering through the glass where the flashing cherry lit up his reflection, his mother in the room beyond, locked in her chair, her back turned, forced to stare glassy-eyed at an empty corner of the room rather than out the window she loved, because Michael couldn't take being seen by her some days, the days when he feared she was still in there, when he suspected the doctors knew what the fuck they were talking about.

He caught a final glimpse of what was left of his mother before lurching down the steep stairs, falling as much as walking, tumbling one flight at a time toward the pavement far below. A car alarm wailed in the distance. Some undead and directionless thing like himself had likely staggered into it, not watching where it was going.

Michael wondered how that was possible, for any of them not to see where they were going. He spiraled down the old fire escape, metal clanging, bouncing off the rails that guided him in one direction only: around and around.

Circles. As tidy and looping as the days were short. How could any of them not see where they were going? They'd been going around and around in tiny circles, had been for years, years that sat heavy in the gut of the living. And this was what made stomachs turn: the weight of all that time wasted. It was the seconds and minutes and hours, the true nectar of life, gorged on hungrily and thoughtlessly, forever indigestible, everyone hungry for more.

8 ❖ Gloria

The wildlife was oblivious to all but the spoils. The human world was dead, but Gloria saw that theirs was still gloriously alive. The pigeons had multiplied. They gathered in noisy flocks and fully claimed a city long held on lease. Swooping in thunderous packs, wings like the sound of flags flapping in a breeze, they followed the bounty of trash that drifted everywhere. They picked at the scattered bones bleaching in the October sun. They stirred reluctantly when the dead intruded and hopped around on fragile legs, picking at the scraps. They exploded upward in fear only for the dogs.

The dogs were newly wild. They were still in the process of returning to their lurking, primal states. When they fought over scraps—tugging at a boot until the leg came away from the hip—Gloria saw herself in them. Many of them jangled with the baubles of ownership. A few dragged ruined leashes through the scrap heap humanity had left behind. They howled in the distance or from within buildings and fenced lots. They growled and snarled at each other, fur matted and hackles up. They scratched and bit at their flanks, their own infestations to deal with. Gloria hated seeing the dogs. Many of the poor creatures looked as though they wouldn't last another day or two. Others would probably thrive.

This was the end of the world, that's what she was privy to. She thought of her brother and sister, thought of Carl in prison upstate, and wondered if their world was ending as well. Maybe not. Not yet. Maybe this island was a wound the rest of America would cauterize and survive. Just a nick, perhaps. Either way, here was a glimpse of the inevitable. The world could stagger on a bit, but here was an early view of the looming fate of mankind.

Gloria remembered classes she had taken in college. She had majored in English, but never got far enough to take the classes she wanted to take. It was all the pre-requisites before dropping out, before trying to make it as a dancer on Broadway, eventually resigning herself to waiting tables, partying, marrying the first guy who knocked her up, staying with him even after the pregnancy failed, even after he was locked away. Before all that, there had been a pre-req, a geology class. She had learned a bunch about rocks and volcanoes, couldn't remember what else. All she came away with was an appreciation of time, for the vast eons that stretched out in both directions.

The dogs and the birds and the rats owned this city. The cockroaches and the gnats and the maggots. Gloria stumbled down the streets toward the hope of another meal and was witness to Armageddon. And it was more peaceful than she imagined. The time stretched out and was filled with life being busy *living*. Humans would die and rot, would shamble around with their arms outstretched groping for the meaningless, and time would stretch out and engulf them like the long roads she'd seen pictures of out west.

Ahead of her rose a barricade of cars. A bus parked across the curb, not by accident. The smell came from the other side, people alive. A pocket of survivors. An oasis of ripe flesh. The barricade rose like the Rockies, blocking out ideas of time stretching off forever. There was this thing to consider. The band of undead pressed against the overlapped cars, and an alarm rang out, a car alarm. Clever if done on purpose, a ring of cars that would sound an alarm when the dead came calling.

Gloria crowded in with the rest. She bumped against the bus, waved her arms at the bright smells in the air that seemed to tinge everything pink and shiny. There were people on the other side. Living people. She was one of the animals fenced out. Gloria knew this, knew what she was, what side of the fence she lived on. And she saw that the end of the world was not quite yet. Some were still trying, banding together, building a fortress of buses and cars in the middle of a crumbling city. Fires crackled, the smell of cooked pigeons, maybe dog, maybe something else.

Gloria sniffed the air, taking it all in, feeling that vast stretch of time soaring out to either side of her, knowing this was but a slice, and that the ruin would come to all else. The end of things. And her kind would hasten it, whether they wanted to or not.

9 ✤ Jennifer Shaw

Jennifer's shuffle, which had grown to three dozen since yesterday, made its way across 59th. The promise of living flesh continued to drift north on a breeze steered by glass-walled canyons. It smelled like dozens of survivors, so many that their fear mixed and blended until they couldn't be told apart. Curiosity as much as hunger seemed to drive the shuffle south. As if any reason were needed for limbs long out of control.

Stepping from the curb, her arms out to steady her diminished sense of balance, Jennifer realized she never came this way anymore, not since she was a kid. The shuffle slid around the cars in the street, startling a flock of birds, and Jennifer felt herself cross an imaginary boundary she didn't even know existed, a separation of two worlds delimited by city blocks and a strip of pavement.

The world she left behind was the one she knew as an adult, living and working on the Upper East Side. And here, the width of a paved river away, Sutton Place, the world of her youth. From one island to another with a few steps. She never came this way anymore.

There was a park on the corner she recognized, a park she knew well. There was a puppy she and her sister had begged for. When the two of them both wanted a thing that badly, they were rarely refused, even when their parents knew better. Likewise, when the two of them disagreed, a stalemate of rare violence formed. She and her sister got the puppy because their wishes overlapped. It remained nameless, referred to simply as "Puppy," because they could not agree on anything more proper.

Jennifer couldn't remember the name she had lobbied for, though it seemed a matter of life and death at the time. All she remembered was how fast it grew. Until it was bigger than they were. Until its name made less and less sense. There, in that park, she and her sister had strained against the leash while Puppy dragged them from tree to tree, chasing squirrels. The allure wore off quickly, as Puppy outgrew its cuteness. She and her sister had realized how much work was involved, that their parents were right, and gradually the dog became their mother's. Which meant their mother didn't have to be alone when she left the rest of them behind.

The view of her childhood park was lost as Jennifer crowded against the person in front of her. It was the same obese man she'd fallen behind a block earlier. She tried not to look. The man's ear and a flap of his cheek hung down from where he'd been attacked. When he turned and sniffed the air with his rotting stump of a nose, she was forced to see his grisly molars, his tobacco-stained teeth, right through his open cheek. Flies had taken up residence in his wound and flew about lazily in the cool air, buzzing his head like some great nest, some fleshy hive. Jennifer imagined they would lay eggs in his flesh. The maggots would come soon for him—she'd seen them writhe on others. She wondered how long before she felt them inside her as well.

Ahead of the man was the woman with no eyes in the bright purple dress. She had been a part of the shuffle for five days. Or was it six? Jennifer had lost count. She was envious of this woman. She could see her walking with both arms out, hands tangled up in the clothes and hair of others, her face a blood-caked mess. While she shuffled along blindly in her purple dress, Jennifer longed to switch places. She imagined the games she could play if the world were black. The sounds of car alarms and the crackling of fires might pierce her imaginary travels, but she could learn to ignore the lesser noises, the hiss of boots sliding across asphalt, the grunts and groans of souls disconnected from their bodies, the screams of the terrified living, the wet ripping sounds and crunching bones of a shuffle feeding—

In perfect blackness, in eyeless darkness, she could make the rest disappear. She knew that she could. There were games her father didn't know about, games she and her sister played under the covers while arguments leaked through walls. But being forced to see what her body saw, to endure the flow of the mob, made it impossible to hide from what she'd become. Even when she managed to dream herself away for a few moments, something awful would rip her back into the here and now with hideous force.

Down the block, her old school loomed into blurry view: P.S. 312. A massive brick structure from the days when things were built with someone else's future in mind. Jennifer tried to focus on the school, but she didn't even have control of what she saw. Not always. The constant hunger meant her vision was forever fixed on potential meat. It left her eyes constricting and warping to bring the wounds of others into view. While she tried to concentrate on the edges of her vision, a director with some sick mind roamed the hurts of the world. And so they passed her old school, which remained a blur, much like her childhood.

A neighborhood with old memories, a few of them good. Why didn't she ever walk this way anymore? What was it about this city, with its endless possibilities, that elicited such limited routines? Was it the fear of the faceless hordes? Was it the allure of the known and the familiar? Or was it mere habit?

Jennifer suspected it was none of these things. She thought she knew why she stuck to a track like a subway train, why her selection of favorite restaurants numbered in the handful, why she shopped and visited the same spots over and over, even the same bench in the same park, so consistently that she knew how and when the shade fell across it, thought she recognized the squirrels, even.

To her, the routine was an inoculation against the daily and constant influx of the lost and bewildered, the baggagedraggers, the upward-gazers, the camera-strangled gawkers. It was this plague, this disease, that her life on rails was meant to protect against. It was the abject terror of feeling like—*of becoming*—a tourist.

A friend of Jennifer's confessed this once, that within a month of moving to the city, she had desperately wanted to be recognized as a local, as someone who now lived there. And she harbored jealousy toward Jennifer for being born in the city, which Jennifer found strange. This friend had divulged another secret: that when tourists asked her directions, even if she didn't know the answer, she just made something up. She would only feel bad after they walked away, as they followed her directions and muttered how nice everyone in New York was. It was easier for her to lead nice people astray than to admit she didn't know her way around, that she was in many ways a visitor as well.

It was hard to judge her friend. Jennifer felt the same desire to both blend in and be recognized, to never glance up at the remarkable buildings for fear of being spotted. She went to the same handful of restaurants and bars where she could bump into people she knew, wave exaggeratedly to a bartender or patron, sprawl out in booths with her laptop and newspaper, and prove that she belonged.

A routine. That's what she had fallen into. Decades on rails. She might hear of a new joint opening up with the best such-and-such, but it was in a part of town she never went to. Not a bad part, just a *different* part. Not her part.

A bodega on the corner came into focus. Her hungry eyes spotted movement inside. Survivors. Her potential food scrounging for their potential food.

The shuffle turned that way, holes in faces where noses used to be sniffing at the air, and Jennifer remembered the store. It had been there as long as she'd been alive. She'd just forgotten about it. She never came this way anymore.

And so she shuffled along, moving toward another feed, a fat man's face hanging open in front of her near enough to worry the flap of flesh might touch her nose, close enough to smell the awful breath leaking out of his clenched but gaping jaw. There was the buzz from one of the flies circling his head, the tickle of it crawling in her ear, another one at the corner of her mouth, and she was unable to swat them away or dig her finger after them.

Laying eggs, Jennifer thought, horrified. Soon, their brood would wiggle within her. They would hatch and grow and feed on her flesh. They would writhe within her, like the man with the hinged cheek and flopping ear.

The itch in Jennifer's ear grew to a great pressure, a pounding agony, an amazing torture to be stomped by such tiny feet. Her body groaned, her voice a wheezing whisper, as the buzzing grew and the flies burrowed themselves deeper.

She screamed in her head for it to stop and prayed for death, but Jennifer shuffled silently onward, no control over where she went, the same as she ever was.

10 ✦ Michael Lane

Michael tumbled down the fire escape. His legs moved on their own, numbly, like the unfeeling stagger of a good high. He was three stories above the pavement when his feet tangled and he crashed into the railing. Bending at the waist, his head flopped forward, and there was a moment of panic and a last desperate attempt to control his limbs before he tumbled over, his heels flying up above his head.

The fall lasted a brief forever. There was the sensation of dropping, wind on his face, body contorting out of control, windows flashing by, and then, finally, interminably, the thud of impact.

The landing was catastrophic. He couldn't twist to soften the blow or pull his feet beneath himself. Both knees struck first, and then his face. Michael felt a tug on his thigh, a deep wound. His body writhed out of control, trying to right itself. Arms flailed like a petulant child told it couldn't have some cherished thing. He could feel powdered bone grind and grit inside his knees as he rolled over.

Putting weight on one leg caused it to buckle, bone hinging where it shouldn't. Michael tried to lie still, but his body made another attempt, less weight this time, balancing on a flopping leg, cracked bone spearing his flesh, his face on fire from the pavement, lips stinging, the taste of his own blood mixing with that of his mother's.

Both knees were crushed. One leg was shattered, his thighbone bending like a second knee, but the pain didn't do shit. Muscles still worked. Tendons were connected to bones, even if bones weren't connected to each other. With spasming jerks, his body worked it out, throwing a leg forward like one of those hinged prosthetics, balancing on a clean break, throwing another leg forward on a crushed knee, balancing, arms out, groans of agony leaking through split lips, the smell in the air of living flesh driving his body forward.

Michael watched through the lens of his soul, a victim of every lanced nerve, the agony horrific. Needles shot through his legs and face. Something was wrong with his abdomen, his stomach cramping and full. At the end of the alley, he saw shapes—people—moving through the parked cars spread across the wide avenue beyond. Moving gracelessly, these other people threw their bodies forward, arms out, shoulders stooped, many of them injured as well, a macabre dance of wounded limbs, a strut of shattered bone.

The pain. It meant nothing. It wasn't a signal to lie still, to stop. It just *was*. A thing. Something to endure. No purpose, except...

Michael noticed something through the burn.

As his body was consumed with this fiery hell and his mother sagged in his guts, he realized the old craving was gone. The withdrawals. They were over. Passed by. Cauterized. Melted through. Ground to ash.

The only pain left was the physical. Nails were driven through him with each hammering lurch. And his other hurts, the ones he always thought debilitating, the ones that kept him on the sofa for days, they cowered in some hidden recess, terrified of this new, sudden, and *real* misery that had wrapped itself around him, squeezing him so tightly that his bones crunched into smaller and smaller pieces, bits of glass slicing him from the inside, needles, the sting of angry nectarless bees.

Out of the alley, Michael emerged broken, dizzy, and aware. He was dead in some ways and alive in others. The sun was high, the rays warming a city that still held the chill from a clear fall evening. Monsters lurched everywhere, following a scent to the next feed, dragging their wounds along with them, oblivious, enduring, or both.

Hesitating a moment, his balance unsure, Michael felt a twinge of control, a sliver of time when desire and deed overlapped, when he found his body doing what he perfectly wished. Just a moment, like a broken clock that twice a day tells the proper time, and then Michael Lane threw a leg ahead of himself. He limped forward, despite his wishes. He merged, blending, joining the others.

11 ✤ Gloria

There were good moments. Somehow, there were moments less miserable than others. The group Gloria had fallen in with might splinter in the swirling breeze, and a small troop would find itself rambling through a park beneath the twittering birds, the air midday warm and the taste of human flesh mostly gone from her mouth.

Even there, in the end of times, when God had taken the righteous from the earth and had left her behind, there were moments less miserable than others.

Central Park brought one such respite. It stood like an oasis, a perfectly rectangular eruption of nature in the center of that mad island with its spikes and spines of concrete and steel. The greenery beckoned. It invited her in with the scent of hidden survivors, this weak smell of fear among the earthy tang of mulch and the mint and spice of untamed plants.

Gloria's small group of bloodstained stragglers splintered among the benches and bushes. Deeper within, a large rock wall confounded a few, the trees dividing the pack like fingers running through tangled hair. The city disappeared, just as the park's designers must've intended. Gloria thought of all those who came here to escape the bustle and noise. Now they came to be surrounded by things alive, to take leave of all the death in the streets, perhaps to find wild mushrooms, trap wildlife, scrounge for food.

Through the mulch and tall weeds, through the last grasses of fall, Gloria trudged deeper. She came to one of the park's many bodies of water: a pond scattered with unmanned boats steered only by the breeze. Gloria watched, mesmerized, while one of the monsters ahead of her steered into the water. The young man sank to his knees, his arms flailing, before tipping forward. He made a splash, writhed for a moment, then disappeared. A duck coasted on the swell he made, its tail twitching in brief annoyance.

Gloria never stopped moving. She continued along the pond's edge, wondering what would happen to that man. Would he remain there beneath the water, the shadows of ducks blotting the sun? For how long? Forever? Or would he float to the surface? Or would his flailing arms learn to swim?

The ripples he'd made faded as Gloria's feet carried her along the rocky shoreline. Trees denuded of most of their leaves reflected in the mirrored surface, tall buildings rising up beyond, one of the buildings on fire and belching dark smoke, the nostrils of a fierce beast. Gloria imagined the man walking along the bottom of the lake, no bubbles leaking out, the depths down there freezing and dark as ink.

Would he die? Was that still possible? Was it possible for her?

She felt afraid for her feet. Concentrating on the breeze, on the smells, Gloria felt fear anew. If the scents wavered, she could be the one splashing in, the one throwing up concentric swells. The thought of the dark and deep, the bitingly cold, it was worse than her fear of a feed. But there was also something like hope there on that shoreline. Maybe there was an end, a completion to what God had begun.

The breeze stirred. It swam like a nearly visible serpent through the trees. Gloria spotted a woman walking through the woods, dragging her leg. The dead were everywhere, fanning out, sniffing and listening, and Gloria prayed:

Dear God, please forgive me. Whatever I've done, please forgive me. Take me, God, with the others. Please don't leave me here.

She tried to think of some forgotten offense, some reason to have been left behind. God knew everything about her. What could she add? How could she feel more sorry?

Please don't leave me here, Lord.

Her shoes crunched through the gravel by the edge of the pond. She imagined herself veering to the side and walking out across the waters, ripples spreading out from her footsteps, and then her soul rising up through the clouds as a grand mistake was corrected. There would be apologies and explanations. Maybe she would discover that this was her penance. She thought of her mother's rosary beads, the quiet prayer she was always whispering, and maybe Gloria had been damned by her father's church, by being raised a Protestant. Maybe it was that Carl's sins in prison were great enough to damn them both.

She shook such thoughts from her head. How many extra days would she suffer in her damnable state for thinking such things? And how many more days for feeling this fear rather than true guilt? And more days heaped on for worrying about that? And that? And so on and forever—

A smell distracted her. It came from the woods, the drift of meat. Gloria's feet chose to put distance between the rest of her and the water's edge. She bumped into a low wrought-iron fence once, twice, before finding the gap that led into the deeper woods. There, through the crunching leaves and scattering of squirrels, a group of her kind had formed, a cluster of the damned. They milled about the base of a tree, arms in the air, rotting noses lifted high.

Gloria looked. She saw the dangling shoes. And then the swinging legs. There was a scabbed knee with a dried trickle of delicious red running down a shin. There were arms wrapped around a mother, who was wedged between the great divide of the tree's largest boughs, fifteen or more feet off the ground. And over the grunts and struggles of the tottering dead rained the whispers of a parent who did not seem to know that those below could still hear, still understand:

"Shhh. It's okay, baby. It's okay."

Lies, Gloria thought, joining the others. She stared heavenward. The woman smoothed the young girl's hair, consoling her. She looked ten or eleven, but starvation took years as well as pounds. The mother peered down, cheeks gaunt, and watched the new arrivals. Gloria felt horrible for these two. Gloria was starving.

The child sobbed. Her feet kicked out of agitation. Or maybe those frail legs had grown so used to running the past weeks that they couldn't stop moving. While they wheeled the air, Gloria circled the tree, her eyes locked on that limb, the smell of the living intoxicatingly near and impossibly far. Here was the manna of her desire, craving it even as she feared it, causing her to wonder, with the hellishness of all that she'd seen and the ungodly predicament of mother and child, not how the two of them had gotten up on that limb and what would become of them, but what Gloria had done to deserve to be there, to be left wandering in circles on that lowly, cursed, and unholy ground.

12 ❖ Michael Lane

Michael balanced on a flopping leg, a limb like a prosthetic, kicking his unfeeling foot forward as split bone bore down on split bone. He moved slowly in this teetering fashion toward the end of the garbage strewn alley behind his apartment building. A handful of undead just like him shuffled past. There was a smell of the living, the smell of meat, new smells instantly understood. Unless these odors had always been there, and now his locked-in state made him newly sensitive to them. Or perhaps not sensitive to them—maybe he had simply become dead to everything else.

Wavering in the street on his busted legs, the air swirling around him, Michael saw that all of New York now resembled his apartment. There was trash everywhere. Cars lay scattered like some god-child had been playing with them before losing interest, before becoming distracted. Several were wrecked, hoods bent, glass everywhere. It was close to noon, and the buildings stood tall without shadow. The pavement held that mild warmness in the middle of a fall day, that brief respite before the chill set back in with the night.

How long since Michael had been bitten? How long since he'd used? It felt like a week ago that there'd been a banging on the door. It had to be the Chinese food, about two goddamn hours too late. Or maybe the bitch down the hall with the rock she owed him.

It'd been neither. A grotesque monster, some kind of a prank, but a bite on his wrist anyway.

Michael could still hear the slammed door, the slobbering noises and the bangs on the walls.

That thing could smell him. It was after him the way he'd gone after the cat, the way he'd gone after his mother.

Michael's stomach was at a boil. He felt clammy and cool. There was a stench in the air, a new reek across a city rife with them, and he suspected he contributed to the foulness.

How long since he'd been bitten?

Michael felt his insides shiver from something like withdrawals, but different. Another itch he couldn't scratch, a new urge wafting on the air along with the smoke from various fires. Several blocks away he could see more monsters like him, like that fucked-up asshole at the door who bit him. They were staggering after one smell, but there was some other scent closer by—

Someone shouted. A person. Someone with lips and a tongue that obeyed the urge to speak.

"Stay!"

Michael wobbled in place. The pain flowed from the broken bones and soothed all his discomforts. Behind him, three men moved from car to car. Wrapped in rags and carrying guns, they looked like terrorists, like those jihad fucks, whatever they were called.

Two guns swung up from behind a yellow cab. The third person moved to another car, trained his gun as well, hissed something, and one of the men moved. They were leapfrogging across the street. Michael could barely smell them. He smelled a hint of something else. Something powerful that he was dead to, so it barely leaked through. He was bad at this, naming flower smells. Those books he had to read in college, always jasmine and honeysuckle and clover and some shit that meant nothing to him. It was one of those smells.

It felt good to move toward the men, to limp at them. The pain in his leg beat the ever-living shit out of the pain in his head. Goddamn, that was something. The pains he'd lived with all his life, and they were pussies to something as simple as balancing on a shattered leg. How about that. People broke legs all the goddamn time. And here he thought his private hell was something special.

The men played leapfrog. Michael tried to keep up. They raised rag-wrapped fists to each other, made hand signals, trained their barrels. They kept an eye on Michael, watching him struggle with his legs, arms jerking for balance, a distant groan dribbling past his lips as he tried to yell at them, to ask them who the fuck they were. Not military, he didn't think. Just people getting by.

They were almost to the corner of the street, moving slowly and methodically, weeks of practice. One of them worked on a door, the other two watching him. Maybe it'd been *Stray* they'd yelled earlier, not *Stay*. Made more sense. They must know Michael couldn't stay. Couldn't control shit. He was a loner away from the herd, a straggler, a new arrival to whatever this was, this sickness throughout the city.

One of the men laughed at something, and his neighbor joined in. They were laughing at *him*, these men in rags. Their barrels shook with humor.

The man by the door hissed at them to shut up, but the others continued to quietly laugh. And Michael saw himself the way he sometimes did when he got high: His mind leapt out of his body and zoomed away until it could peer down at his shell, see his place in the cosmos, see how others might see him, not passed out on the floor or the couch this time, needle still embedded in his arm, dipped in a blue river, just dangling there. Not in the bathroom, throwing up in the shower, on himself, the water having run cold an hour ago. He was in the streets, cars scattered, some shit on fire somewhere, jerking his arms so he didn't tip over, propped on one busted leg and another that was mangled.

The world lurched to the side with awareness of just what kind of shit he was in, that this was *real*. His stomach strained against his jeans, felt tight and bloated. Something warm ran down his legs, the taste in his mouth foul, fur and flesh caught in his teeth.

Michael pissed himself. The barrels shivered with laughter.

And Michael had this sudden sense that *other people were people like him*. Like he used to be. That was him behind the car, joking with a friend, peering down that barrel, wrapped in rags soaked in perfume, playing like characters in a video game. That was him making fun of a sick fuck who couldn't even stagger down the street without looking a fool. That was his sister over there, hair curling out of those rags, one of her boyfriends busting into a supermarket, doing the cool shit of surviving, of living, rather than locked away in some fleshy cocoon, some goddamn filthy apartment.

Someone raised a fist. Michael knew that meant they were about to move. More leapfrogging. The door to the building swung open, a mummy's arm waving the others his way.

One of the jokesters turned and jogged toward the supermarket, clover or honeysuckle or some shit stirring in the air. Michael shuffled down the middle of the street, a patch of open pavement, a man in rags pointing a gun at him from behind a cab and laughing.

"What?" Michael wanted to shout. *"Who the fuck are you? You don't know me. You don't know what I've been through."*

The two friends by the door hissed at him to come. The man behind the cab raised his fist, and then his hand returned to the gun, steadied it as the barrel lowered, Michael getting closer by the inch.

Laughter. And then it stopped for a moment. The barrel did as well.

A thunderclap. A roar. A flash and a geyser of smoke.

And the only leg Michael had left, the only thing he could prop himself on—this was taken from him as well. Hot steel chewed through the better of his two knees like a charging dog. Michael's leg shattered. His leg was blown clear away.

He hovered there a moment before the fall, the echo of the gunshot screaming down New York's perfect canyons, and then, wobbling on split bone and no bone at all, Michael crashed helplessly toward the pavement. Above him somewhere, off to one side, howling laughter erupted before disappearing into the city's steel walls—and there he went with his friends, rushing inside for good times, for laughing times, for the plunder and play, the life he thought he was living even as he pissed it all away.

13 ❖ Jennifer Shaw

Jennifer found herself in the middle of the shuffle. Along the edge, one had a better view of the world. You could get a sense of where the group was heading, whom they were after, see survivors making a dash or boarding up windows. In the middle, all you saw were your decaying neighbors, a menagerie of wounds and disgustingness, up-close horrors like a Google image search of *festering pus*.

Moving along in the middle of a large shuffle also meant never knowing where the victims of a feed came from. You never saw how they began. There would be a distant smell of fear, the gurgling sounds of hungry rage, an excited quickening of the pace, some tottering stampede.

If the living put up a fight—and Jennifer always prayed they would—the fallen members of her shuffle would appear on the pavement with their heads bashed in or blown away. Sometimes their arms and legs would still be moving, clutching and kicking at the feet sliding by, tripping up their fellow undead.

The latest feed began like so many others: a scream and the smell of someone surrounded, the raw odor of a living person who knows that death is upon them, the starving snarls of anticipation.

Jennifer found herself hurrying with the rest of the shuffle, many of the limps growing exaggerated, rotten heads bobbing up and down. There were no lucky zombies to trip over along the way. No souls spared the waking nightmare. No gunshots, the promise and hope of a stray bullet. The victim of this feed wasn't the result of a group fight, just someone who had gotten in the way. Had stumbled or had become cornered. A shriek while they were still able, and then the maddening smell of blood and meat released into the air.

Part of Jennifer hoped the meat was gone before she got there. She was most happy when the other half of her mind, the mad half, was starved and weak. She would rather starve, rather feel empty inside, suffer the gnaw of her gut, than watch herself eat.

This, unfortunately, was not one of those times. Jennifer swam through the shuffle until she came upon a mother with her son, neither swift enough to get away. Maybe the boy had fallen, tripped, and the mother did what any mother would: made the mistake of going back for him.

Despite her revulsion, Jennifer fell beside the fat man with the flopping ear and began to feed. She tried to look away, to look anywhere else, but her body was locked rigid and wide-eyed on the still-warm flesh, on the purple ropes that came unknotted from the woman's belly. The young boy was torn in two. The mother's face jerked, mouth open, eyes unblinking, staring up at the clouds overhead. This was what the world had become.

A warm and tangy taste filled Jennifer's mouth, blood running down her throat, down her chin, the feeling in some dark recess of her soul like a flash of guilt-ridden joy, this radiance of a hunger sated, emotions from the black side of her bleeding over into what little of her old self remained.

Her hands pawed through the woman's remains, dozens of other hands fighting, teeth gnashing, a leg dragged away by several others, the flesh between pulling apart like Silly Putty before snapping. Jennifer was forced to witness it all. To smell it and consume it.

She bit into a length of intestine, raw shit in her mouth, and still could not physically gag, could only recoil emotionally. She tried reciting the alphabet backwards, tried singing long forgotten songs in her mind. She repeated the first few lines of the Canterbury Tales, but what was stronger than this? What mental effort or childhood game could silence the gluttonous undead, could overpower the stench of an opened body, the taste of human waste?

The rear of the shuffle crowded in, jostling her, rubbing up against her flesh, fighting for scraps. Jennifer urged these competitors forward. *Eat, eat*, she cried to herself. They were all that she pulled for. Her own body was the enemy.

She and the fat man fought over an unidentifiable scrap. He was larger—and won. Jennifer watched the red prize spill from the open wound on his neck, empty and yellowed teeth chomping on nothing, a satisfied vigor in his dead limbs.

And the awful truth, the glaring obviousness of it all finally struck her. Jennifer's gaze met the fat man's, their eyes locking for a moment, and she saw, somehow, through that soulless window and into the mind beyond. Past this blood-smeared face, the happy chewing, the twitching arms, was a frightened man. Trapped. Terrified. Imprisoned like a passenger in that roaming form, looking out like a frightened child between cracked blinds at the scary world beyond.

It wasn't just her.

And with an explosion of clarity the entire shuffle came to life around her. She thought of the thousands of trapped souls scrambling for sanity, clutching their private pasts, forced to watch what they'd all become. And the crushing blow of this was like a bat to Jennifer's head. There was a *man* in that fat face with its hideous wound. A man like her who remembered this city, remembered what they *used* to be. Jennifer wanted to call out, to wave, but didn't know how. And she wondered if *he* knew she was in this body of hers, watching him, knowing him. Was he scared of her? How bad were her own wounds? What did he see?

She couldn't know.

And in the same instant that Jennifer Shaw realized she wasn't alone, she felt it more powerfully than ever before. They were *all* alone. All in their individual hells. No escape, no hope, no control. No way of even saying to each other:

I see you in there.

14 ✤ Gloria

It sounded like hands digging in buckets of popcorn, like Velcro pressed together and ripped back apart, all those fingernails gouging and scrambling against the bark of the tree. Gloria jostled with the pack beneath the limb. Mother and daughter sat above, quietly crying and whispering false hopes, cornered like cats by a pack of dogs.

There was no escape, Gloria saw. For the past few hours, she had studied the predicament of the two women, and there was no escape. Not for any of them. This was what frightened her the most: The left-behind souls scrambling at the trunk were just as trapped as the starving couple in the tree. And a steady trickle of the blood-crusted meat-eaters was shambling through the woods to cluster beneath that limb. It was like ants spilling down a slippery funnel they couldn't get back out of. They were all trapped, every one. They would be until those women on that limb starved to death or lost their balance, until they were either consumed or their meat rotted in death and stopped smelling like sweet succor.

This was not a problem Gloria had foreseen. The living simply did not do this, they didn't hover almost within reach, neither running nor dying. They survived or they were consumed. They got away or they passed through the guts of the damned. One side or the other won, never a stalemate.

Not a stalemate, Gloria thought. Purgatory. Trapped in the in-between. They were a lot like Gloria in that way, and she wondered what they had done to deserve this. Something, obviously. The Lord was just, all sins accounted for. They had all done something to be trapped there.

Hours went by, thinking such circular thoughts. Gloria circled that tree, which she thought was an oak. She bumped into the others and took her turn scratching the rough bark. She clawed at the air and groaned at the nothing, secretly privy to the voiced fears and panicked whispers that drifted down from above.

And Gloria prayed for deliverance. She thought of that shoreline she had walked down hours before and wondered if turning toward the water, toward the thing she feared in that moment, may not have been the better choice. Wasn't this her lot? Her life? Was this the lesson God was attempting to hammer home?

Gloria kicked through the dry leaves and mulled over the times she'd felt both trapped and safe. Trapped in marriage, even after the baby was taken from her, even after her husband was locked away. The sin of divorce was that frigid lake, and so she circled Carl for years and years, pawing at the empty space around her.

A job she hated, turning over rooms, making bed after bed, picking up scattered towels and restocking stolen toiletries. Every day, tiptoeing through wrecks that looked more like robberies than a night's stay, dealing with creepy men who put signs out for service, but were still in there, sometimes a towel around their waists, pretending to be startled, sometimes wearing nothing at all. Men sent by the devil to harass her, tell her she was pretty when she knew better, offer her money for unspeakable things.

A job she hated, but change was the other way. Applications and learning something new were the icy deep.

The city was a funnel. Gloria looked around her, something she secretly did on the subway. All different colors, different backgrounds, all the accents. Ants drawn to honey, but they can't get away from the city. They land with their parents or bring their own children, get that first job, learn to drive a cab or flip a room, and never leave.

This was her sin, Gloria thought. God had given her command of her feet and had set her on the shore of life, and she had chosen to live the least. She had always chosen to avoid her fears, had shrunk from the daunting and the risky. And what had her Savior done? Had he walked away from the challenge, or had he strolled across the water knowing he would not sink?

Gloria let out a frustrated gurgle, a prayer to Saint Anthony, the liberator of prisoners:

Tear down my prison walls. Break the chains that hold me captive. Make me free with the freedom Christ has won for me. Amen.

She prayed to Saint Leonard, the patron Saint of captives, slaves, and all those held against their will:

Pray for those like me in prison, St. Leonard. For those forgotten in prison, pray for them. Amen.

Gloria prayed for herself, for her own plights. She prayed for someone to grant her the courage. She prayed for deliverance, for rescue, for something to break her free of the cycle in which she'd long been trapped. She prayed that she could do it all over again, that she might head west and live in a small town, find a different job, a good man, try once more to start a family, to have a child or two or four. She prayed and prayed the same prayers, her words running out, forming small loops, memorized verse, begging and begging for release as she circled that tree, bumping into so many others, but giving little thought to them at all.

15 ✤ Michael Lane

Michael's balancing act came to an end, his good leg chewed away by the shotgun blast. He tipped forward, stumbling on the flopping lower half of his shin, which bent and twisted until his foot was pointing backward. His face struck the pavement, his discombobulated arms fluttering uselessly by his side, too uncoordinated to break his fall.

He waited for death. He waited for unconsciousness. His sister was there, bending down, reaching out a hand to him—but it was the fever of sobriety. It was a construct of the pain.

Screams came out as gurgles, bloody drool dripping onto the pavement, a flashback to a thousand nights spent hugging a toilet, the taste of bile in one's mouth, the smell of urine, realizing he'd wetted himself in his stupor.

A new low. This was always his thought, every weekend in college getting smashed and regretting it, every Monday morning hung over in class, promising he'd never do it again. By Thursday, such promises were forgotten. By Saturday, he hated himself once more.

Michael's limbs stirred. He screamed internally as hot steel was pressed to a dozen unnatural joints in his legs. His dumb physical self was trying to stand. His unthinking body was telling the rest of him, a friend who knew better, *that he was good enough to walk.*

Propped up on his arms, he felt the ravenous puppeteer that had a hold of his will command his legs forward, foot twisting unnaturally, the sensation of his skin being tugged as it was the only thing holding him together.

Several times, his body tried to get his mangled feet beneath him. Each time was a new height of sensation, bones like shattered glass grinding together, the crunch and pop of thin shards giving way, a dull roar reaching his ears that he vaguely recognized as his own voice. He was unable, even, to mercifully pass out.

Eventually, his drunken body learned what the brain could not tell it: walking was out. It would never happen again.

Michael lay still a moment, appreciating the end of the struggle, the throbs and electricity soaring and coursing through his body. This could be the end. Please, let this be the end. There would be no more regrets. No chance at anything regrettable. *Come for me, darkness!* he screamed in his mind. And he could hear it. He could hear that reading voice that used to pop in his mind when he was forced to stare at books, that ability for the talking side of his brain to send signals over to the hearing side.

Fucking die! he yelled to himself. He yelled it so loudly that he could hear it in his mouth, in the depths of his throat, like a swallowed whisper.

He thought of his sister. His mother, whom he carried inside of him. He was losing it, but this time to clarity. He laughed madly and silently at the thought of his mother carrying him inside her belly, and now she was inside his, a mystical torus, a fucking Möbius strip of mother and son in each other's guts.

What if he'd *never* die?

There was a scraping sound nearby. Michael's sideways view of the world was momentarily full of dragging feet, and then a yellow cab, pavement, and a building where survivors must be laughing and raiding, scrambling for food, popping another shell into a shotgun.

Passing minutes. Dragging feet. The undead surrounded him, and then moved on. They were summoned perhaps by the blast that took his good leg or by the smell of the living, a smell that lingered somewhere beyond the persistent pain—

More scraping. The world lurched forward. Michael spilled out of his agony-filled haze and realized he was *moving*. Something was dragging him along.

And then he felt it. His arms reaching out, fingernails finding the rough nicks in the city streets, fingernails bending backward and breaking as he hauled himself forward, fingernails dragging him along after the others.

No.

Fuck no, Michael screamed.

Oh, fucking no dear God please fucking kill me now, he yelled.

And nobody heard him. All that remained was the scraping noise, hands clawing at the pavement, a body learning to adjust itself to this new and crippling low as it figured out how to move, how to go out and seek ever new and deeper valleys in which to crawl.

16 ❖ Gloria

Morning came, and birdsong filled the air around all the trees but one. Unlike the squirrels, which would burrow through the leaves by undead feet, the birds chirped warily and from a distance. When they did swoop in, it was only briefly to pick maggots from a cheek or eye socket. They would perch on a shoulder and pluck a morsel or scrap of rotten flesh, maybe a torn bit of fabric for their nest, and then flap away to a far branch. While they preened and ate and squawked at the world, another leaf would lose its precarious grip and drift down around Gloria and the others.

It had been an especially cold night for all of them. Frost lay in patches, the browning leaves looking as if dusted in sugar, the uncut grass and tall weeds adorned with frozen crystals. Gloria wasn't sure how the mother and child in the tree had survived the bitter cold, but they were already moving about on the broad limb. The mom directed her child into a patch of sunlight that managed to lance through the distant buildings and silent trees to warm a spot of air. Their whispers leaked through chattering teeth.

Gloria had spent much of the night drifting in and out. She remembered coming to and hearing the sobs, which she assumed at first to be from the child, but it was the mother crying. She also saw the pack had grown in number. The tree was one of those crab pots the poor animals could crawl into but never get out of. Gloria and the rest would be there until the couple starved and rotted, until the appetite was gone, the scent dissipating.

It was bitingly cold, and the evidence formed in puffs of false breath, the undead groaning in hungry frustration, the woman and young girl above adding their own shivering clouds to the air.

Gloria circled beneath them. She watched as the mother seemed to succumb to the stress and cold, as she lost her mind. It took a moment to realize what she was doing, that she was stripping herself bare in the morning chill. With her chin lifted toward the promise of a meal, Gloria followed, curious and confused, as the woman tore her thin shirt into strips and began twisting them together. She was talking to her daughter as she worked, explaining something, some kind of plan.

Whispers of a plan made Gloria feel torn. There was the thrill of maybe witnessing an escape, perhaps a dash down the creaking and frost-slick limbs, a daring swing or jump to a neighboring tree. Some plan that relied on racing naked ahead of the stumbling pack, running through the woods still dappled in darkness, hoping to avoid the promise of a roaming bite.

Gloria felt the allure of such daring and guile. She also dreaded the loss of a meal, no end to her infernal hunger, and all those days wasted following their scents.

Strips of clothing were tied together. A belt. Torn and threadbare jeans, much too large. The mother worked in her underwear fifteen feet above Gloria's head. It was the daughter's turn to cry. While she sobbed, her mother looped the knotted fabric around the limb on which they crouched. They were both sobbing. The mother stroked the girl's hair, caressed her cheek. Gloria could see them shivering. Maybe she imagined the blue cast to the woman's naked skin. Perhaps it was real. How they survived the night, she couldn't understand. With her clothes off, Gloria felt she could see every bone in her emaciated body.

"Shhh," she said, consoling her child. "It's okay."

She arranged the improvised rope around her daughter's neck, adjusting it as if getting her ready for school. The girl's thin arms held her mother's wrists. Bits of bark rained down from their movement on the limb.

"I love you," the mother said. The words were interspersed with sobs.

And before Gloria could process what was happening, before she could fully wake, there was a final kiss on the forehead, a scrambling of thin arms as the child realized what plans her mother had for their escape, and then a painful shove out into the open air, the crunch of rope on bark, the yank and pop of a young neck, and then bare feet swinging in the frosty air, the last of the leaves from that great bough leaping to their deaths, shaken off by this disturbance in the tree.

Gloria circled beneath the girl, horrified. A police officer waved at the air, the flesh hanging just out of reach, the child slowly spinning as the twisted rope settled.

There were curses above, the mad screech of a woman at the end of a more figurative rope, the yell of anger at the world that Gloria secretly longed to erupt with, that sort of anger with a silent, invisible, and cruel God that bubbles up with every injustice, every heartbreaking loss, every turn of bad luck. Screams instead of whispered prayer. A woman's throat working and yelling all that needed saying.

Gloria's gaze was lifted to the heavens, to this brave mother, and she saw that the curses and screeches were not directed at any God, but rather at the demons below, the hellspawn she had joined.

More leaves fluttered from their weakening stems as the mother pushed off. And with a great leap, she threw herself out of her misery, not enough rope for the both of them, and Gloria, unable to resist, horrified, dove in with the others and claimed her share. And as she fell on the brave soul, something snapped. Some sinew or thread in her brain, whatever it was that anchored her to sanity, she felt it snap and knew, with righteous surety, that God made no mistakes. He had left her there for her sins, for not being perfect enough. This was her damnation, her eternal reward.

She fought her way through the feeding pack and lowered her face toward the mother's screams. Her first bite was of gaunt and trembling cheek, flesh tearing away. She chewed the mouth of this fallen woman, the rubbery lips, hungry for the mind inside. Hungry for it, even as she lost her own. Even though she was, as ever, unaware that anyone resided there. Unaware that anyone other than her suffered at all.

17 ✤ Jennifer Shaw

It was early morning when the shuffle entered the killing zone. Jennifer had heard the echoing cracks the day before, had wondered what was going on. It sounded like sticks of dynamite the way the noise reverberated off the high walls of glass and steel.

They crossed 23rd heading up Sixth Avenue, leaving the heart of the Village where dormitories lay scattered amid office buildings. There had been a feeding the night before, a bizarre scene where a man, obviously half-starved, had burst out of a ruined pizza shop and had thrown himself into the shuffle, screaming and senseless. It was as though he had given up and couldn't stand the waiting. A depressing thought, but Jennifer's father had taught her how to create stories to give a positive spin to any bit of news. In her mind, the man's mad act had been a noble sacrifice, a distraction while his family fled through the back of the parlor. She pictured them dancing through the streets toward a silent helicopter, a soldier's gloved hand extended, the wind of the rotors kicking up the yellow dress of the man's young daughter, a stuffed animal dragging from her tiny, clenched, and terrified fist.

More games, these little fictions. Stories of what her mother was doing now. Always the fantasy of scanning faces on the walk to work, looking up and down the subway car, seeing her there reading a book or clutching an umbrella, or maybe watching her in turn, smiling.

Little fictions. That's what her father called them. Not lies, just stories to twist the brain into a new shape, to allow the light to spill in with a different color, to throw rainbows instead of shadows. If only he had warned Jennifer how exhausting fictions could be. They were as addicting as they were difficult to keep straight. And when you spent your entire day looking forward to sleep, to those broad moments before you drifted off when you could exist anywhere, a lottery winner, the owner of an island, the last person on earth, the center of a loving family, it didn't make reality more bearable. It made it dull and uninteresting. A slog. A mindless shuffle.

These little fictions, games her father used to play. Jennifer thought of her sister, wondered what had happened to her. Even though her fingers were growing numb with rot, maggots writhing beneath the wound in her wrist, she still imagined she could feel her sister's hand, could hear her voice, could skip through the past and away from the cruel world.

Crossing 23rd, the head of a woman further up the shuffle exploded. They were ranging back over the same city blocks they had already crossed before, passing through silent intersections with dead stoplights that swayed in the breeze, and the head of a woman limping not far ahead of Jennifer simply erupted in a shower of dull gray mist.

What life remained in the woman evaporated. Her body sagged sideways to the ground, the step she had been taking unfinished, just the wobble of a planted knee, a jerk of her arms, what little was left of her head lifted toward the clouds, and then the rest of the pack was shuffling around her, the smell of her dead meat doing nothing for their hunger.

The crack of the rifle came much later, after the woman lay supine in the street. It brought to mind days Jennifer had spent in Central Park, lying in the warm grass, men with unathletic bellies hanging over their belts as they played ball on the dirt diamonds. In the distance, their bats smacked the softballs over feeble leapers with open gloves, the sound coming well after the sight.

The next shot was off-center. It sliced away a woman's crown, a half-cap of hair and skull, a gray mass beneath. The woman's soul left this grateful opening and soared up as her body crashed down. There was a crack in the air that echoed between the buildings, a stick of dynamite. Jennifer felt a mix of emotions as the shuffle trundled along, sniffing the air. There was fear, fear of true death, of parting with her thoughts forever. She was trapped in that rotting body, yes, and dead in so many ways—*but still aware*. She still had her games, her little fictions. Could these suddenly be taken from her as well? Would she want them to be?

It was like being a prisoner, someone with a life sentence with no chance of parole being told by a nurse that she might have but moments to live. How was she to feel about this? Panic? A sense of looming escape? Jennifer's mind whirled with the sudden implications of death popping up among the already dead. Her torment took a new shape. If she had moments left to live, were there any thoughts she would want to have before she went? Any words to the gods she didn't believe in? Any prayers to those she would never see again? The interminable minutes of her infinite days now felt like precious moments, little jewels. The woman directly in front of her took the next bullet in her shoulder and spun around, arms rising from the centrifugal pull as she twirled. Crack-pow! None in the shuffle flinched. Maybe they were also silently praying for and dreading the next one.

This was what a death sentence felt like, Jennifer realized. She was walking down a prison aisle, cages on both sides of her, like Central Park Zoo. She was walking to her death, unable to control her legs, terrified and resigned. This was what it felt like.

The woman who had been hit and spun around had a new jagged wound to live with. She straightened herself and trudged forward with the rest. Another hit, another excellent shot, Jennifer both spared and cursed. Where was this person with the gun? Why shoot them from a distance? And how did they choose? Would she be next?

Her feet dodged around one of the victims of their own accord. All women, Jennifer realized. Four in a row.

The shooter knew. He had to. Or was it a she? A sympathizing woman or some kind of gentleman. Jennifer became convinced of this as an elderly woman in a nightgown with a horrible neck wound was the next to go. There was an eruption of blood, a warm mist on Jennifer's cheek, and then the woman's body sagged straight to the pavement like a fuse had been removed.

Someone was sparing them this torture. They had limited ammunition. Couldn't save them all. Someone knew. Not those army pricks who flew by with their hazard suits on, watching, watching. They probably had orders. Don't kill civilians. As if that's what any of them still were.

But this angel with her long barrel of release, with gifts of lead as valuable as gold, these bullets that could transmute the half-dead into the full, she had watch over them.

Jennifer's fear vanished. It was the intentions that warped her mind, twisting shadows into bright ribbons of color. The shooter was up there crying, wiping tears from her eyes, using a skill her father had blessed her with on a farm out west, releasing poor creatures from the half-grip of death every time she pulled the trigger—a nice little fiction.

Another soul was released, a cloud of brains raining down, splattering the others, the delayed echo of a bang, the crack of prison walls crumbling, the resounding boom of freedom.

Sounds. Sounds that came late. Sounds Jennifer Shaw never heard for herself as they came, singing through that mad, mad air, to release her.

Part II ✦ Dying for Seconds

Chiang Xian • Dennis Newland

18 ❖ Dennis Newland

Dennis sat in a pile of cereal boxes while the others stacked food in shopping carts. Cans rattled to the ground one aisle over. In front of him, little sacks of organic coffee rustled on the shelf as his girlfriend Lisa dug through something on the other side. Dennis looked down at his arm, pulled his hand away from the sleeve of his denim jacket. It was dark and sticky with blood. He should tell somebody. He should tell somebody. He should have told them back when he still could.

A cart squeaked past, little wheels spinning, a crushed box of Cheerios wedged under the front bar. Matt stopped and grabbed a few boxes, threw them on his pile of canned goods. "You okay, dude?"

Dennis jerked his head up and down. He could still do that. Maybe he could still speak if he really had to. He hoped he didn't have to. His jaws felt locked together. Stiff.

"That shit was close back there. I thought we were goners for sure this time."

More jerking of his head up and down. Matt stooped and grabbed a box of Captain Crunch. "I like this stuff. Good without milk." He glanced over at Dennis. "You think we'll ever taste fresh milk again? Or just that Parmalat crap for however long we've got left?"

Dennis tried to shrug. He couldn't tell if he succeeded.

"Ah, fuckit." Matt threw the box in the cart, adjusted the strap he'd rigged to his shotgun, and pushed his spoils down the aisle. "Better get your head together and grab some shit," he called over his shoulder. "You ain't eating nothin' of mine!"

Dennis was left alone with his sticky sleeve. A bag of coffee tumbled off the shelf across from him and landed with a sad thud on the ground, the contents spilling out in a brown avalanche. Lisa was still digging through something on the other side. He could hear her cussing about the batteries in another iPod running dry. They were going through them like packs of gum. Stupid.

He looked down at his arm.

So fucking stupid.

It was getting more and more difficult to move. He had assumed it would be like a light switch when it came, like the Incredible Hulk turning green and ripping his shirt off, some kind of instant morphing into his own permanent Mr. Hyde. But it had started with a slow paralysis, a gradual fatigue that turned into frozen limbs. He could move his wounded arm if he wanted to—he was pretty sure he could lift it up over his head if he really wanted to—but he couldn't make himself *want to*. Staring down at it, Dennis tried to give his own body a weak command. It felt locked. Pinned. He tried harder. Some part of him was still there, was telling him that if he produced a sudden burst of energy, if he just tried *hard* enough, it would be like breaking out of some kind of packed sand.

That's what this was. It was the time his older brothers had buried him in the sand at Virginia Beach. Everything had been funny until he wasn't sure if he could get out or not. They would've made fun of him if he had panicked and tried, but he would die if he couldn't be sure. So Dennis would twitch and wiggle just enough to crack the sand, enough to see if he could still move, and his brothers would laugh and pack it back down, slapping the ground with the flats of their shovels, making the cool sand tight against his chest.

When the sand had been up to his neck and Dennis had realized he couldn't move at all, he'd gotten scared. He had begged them, tears running down his face, salt in his mouth, to please dig him out. And they had laughed. Laughed until his screaming had summoned their mother from the water and their scowls had told Dennis that he would never live this down.

For the second time in his life, Dennis couldn't move. He couldn't lift his hand. Couldn't even twitch his little finger.

He sat there among the cereal boxes, terrified. This time he wouldn't cry. He couldn't cry. He wasn't able.

But then his head moved. It moved of its own accord. Someone else was doing it, pulling strings. And the coffee, the open bag of spilled coffee sitting across from him—Dennis couldn't smell it anymore.

He couldn't smell the coffee. But he could smell *Lisa*.

19 ✤ Chiang Xian

There was meat hanging in the window. Chickens strung up by their necks, pigs wrapped in twine with their little hooves in prayer, fish frozen mid-dive, their dull scales cracking off and fluttering to the ground like silver blossoms. The meat was rotten. The air in the tiny shop was heavy with the stench of it after being locked tight for days and days. Clouds of flies gathered and maggots squirmed. The meat had long since ceased to be appetizing.

Two chairs lay tipped over beneath the meat, old and ornate chairs of carved wood. The shop owners had used those chairs to hang their daily offerings and to adjust the signs on which prices fluctuated daily. Chiang Xhen now roamed that shop in meandering circles, bumping into tables, her inhuman and lonely grunts filling the darkened space, her young eyes occasionally falling to the fragile chairs lying on their sides, her thoughts drifting toward her parents.

The crowded city made for a strange life for a young Chinese girl. Her parents had been born in China, whereas she had been born in this tiny microcosm, this span of city blocks made to look like someone else's home.

Sure, she got out of Chinatown occasionally, but not often. Her parents took her to museums and concerts. They stood before large canvases while her mother showed Chiang how other people made brush strokes, what a hand both confident and relaxed could produce. Both of her parents stressed hours of practice. There, look at how that woman in the first chair plays violin, how her hand lays over to the side with just the edges of her fingers sliding up and down the strings.

Chiang complained after one concert that she was only ten, that it hurt her fingers to twist them that way. And when they got home that night, Chiang's mother uncovered her own feet and pointed to them, and Chiang kept future discomforts to herself.

Her parents had been born in China and had brought much of it over with them. But it was a warped version of home, Chiang discovered. The more she talked to her friends, the more she found that her parents held in their hearts a fantasy version of their homeland. Chiang was now eleven, and had only that year discovered that dragons weren't real. They never had been. It made her question the dinosaurs from that museum, too.

At her one-room school over a noisy restaurant, with the banging of pots and pans in the background, they learned a lot of politics. Her teacher didn't know English. She spoke more of the news in China than she did of the city in which they lived. Chiang learned without meaning to that she was lucky to be alive. Back home, her parents may have decided to not keep her. But here, she could have all the brothers and sisters she wanted.

She didn't argue with her teacher, didn't mention her mother's feet or the way her father looked at her with sadness. She had only begged for a little brother once. Her parents had yelled at one another all night, making it impossible to sleep. So whenever her teacher spoke of such things, Chiang gazed out the window at something else.

Usually, it was at the bold stripes on the flags of Little Italy, which every year her people encroached more and more. When she mentioned this to her father once—that she felt badly for the Italians—he had shrugged. Pounding a flank of meat with his wooden hammer, he had explained to her that some people care more about where they come from than others. He told her to feel sorry for them about *that* while he hammered the meat with more anger.

Chiang had felt sorry for her father that day, and for the meat.

She made another circuit of the shop, her parents' shop. She had never been so hungry in all her life. The days had gotten away from her—not for lack of counting or so grand a number, but because her mind wandered as it grew dark and light again outside. Strangers occasionally pressed against the glass, eying the meat, deciding it wasn't for them. This much hadn't changed. Tourists, turning their noses up at delicacies. Laughing and taking pictures. Only, they didn't take pictures anymore. They paused with their horrible wounds. The disgusting display was in reverse, now. And then they lumbered onward, these tourists who had become grosser than the things they used to mock.

Chiang wondered how long this would last, how long before everyone died for good. She ran that last day over and over in her head. School had been cancelled suddenly, parents arriving for their children, people running in the streets. Only, they hadn't been screaming. That scared her the most, the wide eyes and slack jaws of the adults hurrying away with their children in their arms. In the movies, they were always screaming as loudly as they could while a Chinese version of Godzilla crushed buildings beneath its scaly feet. Instead, there had been silence, which was unnerving because it wasn't right. The people simply scattered, legs hurrying, no time for screams at all.

Or maybe they didn't want to draw attention. The sick were already in the streets. It was difficult to see them, for they moved slowly. They didn't stand out. Not until you bumped into them, looking for your parents, fighting the crowds to get home, when a kind stranger takes your hand, bends down to see if you need help, and bites off your fingers.

Chiang made another lap of the shop. She had never been so hungry before. Even waiting until the last customer was served before her mother made something in the back had never been this bad. Nothing had. She'd lost count of the days spent circling the shop, but it had been three since she'd had anything to eat. Three days with the hunger driving her mad, the feeling of her insides turning out.

A newspaper fluttered by outside and pressed itself to the glass. It was like a tourist, peeping in. Headlines from those last days were spread across its face—news of an outbreak entirely under control. Until it wasn't. Chiang wondered what was happening in China. She thought of her school teacher and all her friends and wondered what had happened to them. As the people passed, she looked for anyone she knew, but they were all tourists.

The newspaper flapped away on the breeze. Where it had pressed, Chinese characters painted with a young and unsure hand could be seen against the fading backlight of another counted day. The characters were supposed to say:

人生. Rénshēng. *Life.*

Outside, it would have read this way. To the tourists, of course, it meant nothing. Just part of the backdrop that lent Chinatown its authenticity. For locals, however, it promised something: healthy ingredients and traditional medicines. Eternal life.

Chiang had laughed when she'd first seen it from the inside. After she had drawn it for the third time, washing off each attempt with a bucket of water and a rag as she attempted to satisfy her mother's exacting standards, she saw what it meant in reverse. From the inside, the brush strokes were backwards. It looked more like:

生人. Shēngrén. *Stranger.*

A stranger life. Life as a stranger. A girl growing up in a home away from home, people she didn't know peering through the glass, taking pictures of and pointing at the delicacies hanging in the window. It was funny how that worked out. Like the characters knew all along that this was coming. A secret only they were privy to.

Chiang laughed in her mind. It was the only place she could laugh or cry anymore. She wanted out. She wanted to run, to skip and shout and scream, but knotted chains hung from the doors of the little shop. Her parents had locked her inside with them, had locked away their one precious girl while she grew sicker and sicker, and they worried more and more.

The sun slanted through the window, casting shadows of words in reverse, and little motes of dust dipped and swirled like fairies with a life of their own. There were two chairs of ornate wood tipped on their sides, catching the sun. The flesh up past the knees might sate Chiang's painful hunger, but she could circle and circle and wave her arms and never reach any more. She had eaten all that she could. She was powerfully hungry and all alone, and meat hung in the window of her parents' shop.

20 ❖ Dennis Newland

"**I**t's the end of the fucking world," Matt had told Dennis, holding out a smoking roach, the day before they'd made a run at the grocery store, the day before Dennis had been bit.

They were still in that office building where they'd been rationing candy bars. They'd just killed a group of survivors eerily similar to their own foursome, another pair of couples thrown together by the nightmare of the world. This other group had been surviving noisily one floor above, carrying on, acting like maniacs. After a long discussion about whether to bring trouble or wait for it to come to them, Dennis and Matt had opted for the latter. They convinced Lisa and Sarah that it was best, that this other group would bring death upon them all. And so they rehearsed and checked their gear and went on the offensive for the very first time.

"It's like that episode of Seinfeld," Sarah had joked, sizing up the two young couples they'd murdered in their sleep. She thought they looked like them. It took some explaining before any of the rest of them got the joke. Sarah was the only one who watched old sitcoms. And besides: nothing much was funny after you'd shot a living person, not while you were digging through their pockets and the bodies were still warm.

Matt was the one who'd discovered the stash. Later that night, he'd held out that roach, the ember fading, telling Dennis to take a hit, that it'd be good for him, that it was the end of the fucking world and to stop being such a pussy.

Dennis had passed. He always did. He mumbled something about asthma, his old and entirely made-up excuse to not smoke. Matt had shrugged and had given life to that ember with a noisy intake of air.

Dennis had no problem lying to friends. He was used to keeping secrets, was skilled at keeping things from others. The sticky wound beneath his sleeve was just the latest. Later that night, while their cubicle fortress filled with smoke, Dennis had found an empty cubicle down the endless row. He had shuffled through the scattered supplies and loose paper like snowdrifts from some weeks-old panic and made himself comfortable in quiet solitude.

He didn't know how to explain to his new friends what getting stoned felt like to him. Hell, he'd been with Lisa for years and had never even told her. He was pretty sure it was a singular reaction, that everyone else must feel something different, but to him getting stoned was a scary place, not a soothing one.

The first time he'd smoked up, he was convinced he would die. The high had lasted for hours, for most of the damn day. He remembered standing in Lisa's kitchen, the cabinet open, hand on the knob, looking at an assortment of glasses. He couldn't remember how he'd gotten there. Must've teleported from the living room. The TV and the laughter from his friends were faraway sounds. He was disconnected from everything.

Later, sitting under a cold shower, praying impatiently for the numbness that had crawled into his veins to crawl the fuck back out, he had watched the hair on his legs wave as the water rained down from the faucet. The hair stirred like the seaweed at the breaker's edge on Far Rockaway, like small arms pushing out of his skin and trying to get his attention, trying to wiggle free. A million dead things buried alive and working to escape their epidermal graves.

Dennis had become terrified that he would always be like that. The pot had permanently dumbed him. Hours later, lying perfectly still on the bathroom floor, his thoughts had begun to clear. He could analyze what had gone wrong. But summoning his thoughts seemed to make his flesh melt away, his body go perfectly numb. And if he tried to move, the opposite happened. He could feel again, but now he couldn't think.

It was one or the other. It couldn't be both. His brain or his flesh, never the two.

Three times in his life Dennis had gotten stoned, and every time it was this choice. He could have his body or his thoughts, but not both at the same time. That little bridge between the hemispheres of his soul got fogged up by the smoke. That bridge had a name. Corpus christi or some shit. Once it was severed, he had to choose. One or the other. Lie still and think or get the fuck up and lose his mind.

So he didn't smoke. Was terrified of the shit. And now it was happening again.

Dennis marveled at the similarities of getting stoned and becoming a zombie as his willpower faded and his arm began to sting less and less. He watched, powerless, as his legs kicked. The movement was a relief, but only for a moment. Cornflakes crunched under the heels of his salvaged boots. And when he began to rise, he did it with the grace of a drunk, with limbs jerking out of control, unsure of themselves.

Dennis was a joystick with its wires crossed. He was playing *Dead or Alive 3*, that fighting game on his XBox, but the man on the screen wasn't pulling off the moves he was sending it. He felt that video game lean, the attempt to urge the action in one direction through willpower alone, but that never worked. Instead, his body lurched across the aisle toward the nearest scent. The player was out of his control. The game had gone to a cutscene, and Dennis had an awful feeling of how it would turn out.

He watched as his arms slashed through sacks of disheveled coffee, digging for Lisa. Some distant and half-sane shard of his former self knew what he was doing. It was as though he'd been locked away in his own skull, some interloper crowding in beside him, and the confines and proximity meant that feeble thoughts and silent screams from the one could bleed over into the other. A monster had taken up residence in his head, and he could read the foul beast's mind, know what it was thinking.

Entire shelves of organic and fair trade scattered to the tiles around his feet. Dark roast and decaf. Coffee from countries where Dennis imagined life continued apace, maybe a news story in Portuguese about an outbreak in Manhattan. Or maybe the entire world was overrun, who the fuck knew?

He heard Lisa calling for him. She was excited, had finally found some special ingredient to this secret meal she'd been promising for weeks. If they ever found a decent store, she'd said, one that hadn't been stripped bare, one dangerous enough on the outside to be rewarding enough within, she'd make him something special.

Well, we made it, Dennis wanted to say, to shout through the shelves. The old part of him wanted to, at least. The new part grunted with hunger and frustration—it had a different meal in mind. This was the part that made him writhe between the tight shelves, forcing his body past rows of coffee. An inhuman gurgle dribbled past his lips, a verbal drool.

Lisa was reaching for something, telling him to come over. Dennis's arms found her arm. The touch was electric—skin meeting skin on a first date, the feel of one's own deadened limb in the morning as numbness wore away into tingles. Dennis's fear for Lisa melted in a flare of endorphins. His worry disintegrated at this discovery, this touch of *meat*, of real food among pre-packaged and processed shit.

Lisa shrieked. Dennis was on his belly like a snake, lurching side to side, sending more cans to their dented fates as he tunneled from aisle eighteen to aisle seventeen.

His girlfriend's screams grew louder and more panicked. It reminded him of all the times he'd hid behind a door before leaping out. Reminded him of the insane pranks of the past week, the humor only boys found funny, the madness wrought of dark survival and fading adrenaline. He would pinch Lisa's calf with the claw of a hand when she wasn't looking, making her think she'd been bit. He'd watch Matt do the same or similar to Sarah, the boys laughing with tears in their eyes while trembling hands slapped at their shoulders, girlfriends calling them assholes, thinking for a moment that the end had come for them.

He didn't know why they did it, why there was this compulsion to strike terror in the hearts of those they loved. More cans scattered as Lisa fought his grip. She was yelling at him now. Her fear had flipped to anger. This was how it worked. Frightened for a moment until she realized it was him, and then just pissed. She tried to pull away, but Dennis wasn't playing this time. He held her arm with a starving grasp, his brain dripping sick thoughts and remnants of guilt.

Why did he ever scare her for fun? He tried to make caveman sense of it. For Dennis, every human drive had to make caveman sense. Where had it come from, this universal oddity? Why did humans do the shit they did? Where did it originate?

Lisa smacked his head as he emerged through the shelves. She begged him to let go. Dennis made zombie noises, grunts and groans of lungs compressed by metal shelving, the air just leaking past his vocal cords. Why did they do it? Did they scare their women as some sort of training? Was it to teach them to never trust any man, even their own? Or was the fear some subconscious attempt to cow them, keep their women feeling helpless and reliant on the protective brawn they provided, like the mafia feigning worry for some shopkeeper who had only *them* to fear.

Dennis didn't know.

He didn't know why they did it any more than he knew why he was doing it for real this time.

Urges.

Caveman shit.

Like eating raw meat. Dennis had never eaten raw meat before, not even sushi. This was his last pre-monster thought as he wrestled his girlfriend's arm to his lips, jaws parting, teeth bared, the anger in her shouts sliding to full-on panic.

She shrieked piercing wails, and Lisa *knew*. She had to know as he bit down on her forearm, a patch of skin he used to kiss, that creamy white with a single mar of a mole that she insisted was a freckle. When his tongue hit her flesh, there was a familiar taste, the salt from weeks of running and not bathing, the hot skin like a day on the beach, the same flavors that tinted their lovemaking. His girlfriend tasted the exact same on the surface.

It was the unfamiliar that lay beneath.

Dennis felt an eruption in his brain like an orgasm. Better. Better than an orgasm. This was what he was wired for. His teeth came together, and Lisa's arm jerked. Desperation. There was desperation in both of them. Panic and starvation were at odds with each other. The desire to eat and to not be eaten. Dennis thought of make-up sex they'd had once, the rough sex. He thought of that first time, when she'd said she didn't want to, but he had convinced her. They were both drunk. He was too far along to turn back. Both naked and willing to do so much, but then him wanted more. More than she did. The drive in him to eat was like that drive to fuck. He would've insisted it was something containable until he'd actually felt it, until he'd gone that far. That far, and you were going all the way. He couldn't stop. Too weak.

Dennis also thought, as he bit down, that teeth were *meant* for this, just not his. He never would've guessed that they could rip flesh. Not *his* teeth. Maybe those of another monster but not his. The flesh of Lisa's arm gave way, his jaw clenching on the softness, and then her skin stopped moving, became tight, could stretch no more, and with a pop, with a sudden orgasmic burst of power, his bottom teeth met his top teeth, a chunk of her arm in his mouth, him chewing.

There wasn't a product on the supermarket shelves as delicious as this. Lisa's safety receded from his mind. What he was doing faded; what he had become made the rest of him cower in fear. Lisa gurgled in pain and staggered backwards, and Dennis latched onto her like a rabid dog. He slid forward, cans bouncing, and emerged from the shelves a different thing than what had entered. He and Lisa were on the ground, rolling around like they used to wrestle, Dennis pulling his way up her body even as he chewed this first glorious taste and swallowed it down.

He wanted her neck. She was yelling for him to stop, begging. The sample in his mouth drove him forward, craving more. This was why he shied away from anything he knew he'd like. One try, and it was over for him. There was nothing for Dennis in moderation.

Lisa cried out for help. She prayed to a god he knew she didn't believe in. Panting for air, yelling for Matt and Sarah, Dennis felt just a hint of guilt. The old him was still in there, sad that shit had gone bad like this. He remembered, even drunk that one night, knowing that he was doing something wrong, that he should stop. But he had driven forward until screams and moans couldn't be told apart, until cries and gasps were the same, until he could convince himself that she was enjoying it too, that she would forgive him, that they would never talk about it, try not to think about it, forget that she had ever begged him to stop.

That was the old him in there, feeling sorry. The rest of him wanted a second hit of this new drug. The rest of him wanted Lisa to shut the fuck up. And as he pulled himself up her chest, he found a way to do both, to get a taste and to silence her. And it amazed him, again, that teeth were meant for this. It was some caveman shit, he thought, as his jaw opened a gushing and hissing hole in his girlfriend's throat. It was some caveman shit as her cries for help were silenced, as her body fell into reluctant submission, he on top of her, getting his way.

21 ❖ Chiang Xian

Chiang was in the back of the meat shop, cornering a rat in her slow and clumsy steps, when the strangers broke in. It was the fifth day of her terrible hunger, the countless day of her imprisonment, and the third time she'd chased after the same rat. It cowered under the old radiator in the back room while someone shattered the glass door at the front of the shop.

Chiang could smell the tiny animal under there. The last two times she'd seen this morsel of brown meat scurry across the floor, her starving body and senseless mind had charged directly after the thing. She had been forced to watch, mad with hunger, as it disappeared into its home behind the cupboard.

This time, Chiang had a better idea. And somehow, her body listened. Like an exhausted arm and trembling brush finally obeying her concentration and producing the perfect stroke, if she thought hard enough on a thing, a direction, her feet seemed to shuffle according to her will. But just barely. And it wasn't easy.

I can do this, she told herself. It was no different than stretching her tiny hands around the neck of a violin. It was just like origami, biting her lip and making sure the edges of the paper lined up just right, to within a hair, that with the drag of a fingernail the folds were crisp and sharp, her miniature paper cranes nearly as good as her mother's. Chiang felt she had studied all her life for this, to corner this one little rat.

She banged into the radiator, and the frightened animal shot off toward her father's back office. Good, good. Chiang shuffled after. Her limbs were too slow to catch the thing by hand. That was true even before she'd lost the fingers on one hand. But there were swifter limbs in her father's office. And so she lurched sideways, frightening the little guy through the open door before following after.

Following after. Chiang thought about an old worry of hers as the rat scrambled beneath her father's cluttered desk. She had this feeling, this nagging sensation even back when her parents were still alive, that her thoughts followed *after* the things she did. They were the echoes of her actions, not the causes of them.

There was something Confucius had once said: *The superior man acts before he speaks*. She didn't think Confucius meant it the way she read it, though. Her fear, as she had struggled to be the perfect girl her parents desired, was that there wasn't any control at all. All men act first and speak after. She felt it herself. She would do a thing and then take credit or make excuses. In truth, she did the thing because she was born to. Because, in that moment, how could she not?

She banged into the desk, just like she had the radiator. On purpose, she thought. She hoped. Almost there. Swifter arms than hers. She could smell the fear leaking out of the rat and figured it was doing much the same as she. Reacting and then feeling something. Some mix of chemicals. Happiness or sadness, fear or desire, these chemicals causing limbs to move toward or away from the good or bad.

Chiang tried to scare the rat from the bad to the worse. She nudged the desk again. The last project her father had been working on—ledgers full of meticulous script, purchase orders for half a dozen vendors—was spread out across the surface just the way he had left it so many days ago. There was an agitated squeak by the wall, the scratch of tiny claws, and then the clack and slam of a metallic arm and the snapping of a tiny neck as a trap long picked clean did its swift work.

Chiang fell to the floor and lumbered beneath the desk. The darkness was no concern; she could smell the crushed flesh like a piece of cracked ginger. Her hands groped for the trap and found it. She pulled the contraption out, the animal's tiny arms still twitching with something that resembled life.

Fists smaller than any intricate crane her mother had ever made unfolded into pink and perfect palms. Chiang only studied them a moment before bringing the trap to her lips. She bit the rat in the belly, still warm and heaving, and her mouth was filled with the hot and sticky scraps picked over and digested by the foul beast, this little survivor. The trap itself was something to chew around. The rest was for her. She peeled slivers of flesh off its body and chewed through bones like chopsticks while someone rummaged noisily in the meat shop.

Chiang stopped chewing and listened. Beyond the moist steam rising from the rat's insides, there was another smell cutting through. Living meat. Something not rancid and spoiled. She could smell them like spices, at least a few of them out there, the odor getting stronger.

Voices.

A whispered hush. The sound of canned goods being scraped off of shelves. There were people in her parents' shop, scrounging for food. Chiang dropped what remained of the rat and shuffled toward the door. She was still hungry. So very hungry. And her limbs seemed to move of their own accord, her mind making excuses, telling herself a story of reasons, as she went along like a puppet.

A family of three. They didn't hear her coming out of the back room, sliding through the red curtains with the green dragons. Chiang saw that they had pressed one of the shelving units against the door. These people had broken in, and her first thought wasn't anger; her first thought was that maybe she could get *out*.

Chiang saw a baseball bat by the cash register, the wide end of it painted and spattered red. It hadn't been there before. She passed behind the counter where her father folded meat into sheets of brown paper, her head just barely poking above. Around the counter and into the store, she nearly bumped into the woman. Chiang saw how the lady's body trembled and froze. The scream came a full breath later, but Chiang was already sinking her teeth into the woman's hip, a mouthful of sweaty-salty shirt and the tender flesh beneath.

Canned goods spilled everywhere. The screaming was hurting Chiang's ears. It stopped as she bit again, the woman going limp and collapsing to the ground, passing out.

A large man shouted. A cry of anguish. He skipped and slid through the piles of canned Chinese ingredients, around the tables and chairs, dashing for the cash register.

The bat. Chiang lumbered to intercept the man. The woman writhed and groaned on the floor like she was having bad dreams. There was a third shape moving in the dimness of the shop. More screaming.

Chiang felt afraid of these people. Maybe they had brought food to her, their untainted flesh. Maybe they had brought escape by shattering what she could not. But they had also brought a lasting death with them, the desire to end her. The man reached the counter and grabbed the bat. Chiang could smell his intentions, his rage and fear. She hurried through the spilled cans, her teeth clacking anxiously on the empty air, arms out in front of her as he reared the bat to the side.

It was a can of asparagus. One of Chiang's senseless feet slipped on the can, shooting her legs out from underneath her, and the stained bat whistled through the air above her head. With a ferocious crack, the bat met the old cash register with its brass buttons and little tombstone prices. Chiang flailed to right herself. Inhuman screams came from the large man. His knees were wobbling like Chiang's. The smell of rage on him grew to a stench. There were sobs behind her from a third person, a shadow. The bat screamed through the air again as Chiang stumbled toward her feet.

The blow grazed the side of her head and came down on her shoulder. Something snapped. Chiang felt her shoulder twist out of place. She kept moving forward. The man was holding half a bat, the splintered ends trembling in his fist. He tried to move backwards, slipped on a can of onions, and Chiang was on him, pulling herself with one good arm and another flashing in pain, the man's hands scrambling to keep her off, until she reached his neck.

Countless days of hunger disappeared in a gushing instant. Blood jetted into her mouth as she tore open the man's neck. It tasted just as her desperate cravings had led her to expect. Warm and vital. Like the sashimi her father would cut and feed her while she worked.

The man's voice left his lips and emerged from his neck, gurgles and bubbles flooding around Chiang's mouth. There was more here than she could eat in a week. She lapped hungrily at the gushing fountain, which gave of itself in throbbing spurts. The two powerful hands scrambling at her face seemed to fade. They pawed listlessly now as Chiang's limbs found new purpose and strength.

A loud crack filled her ears, her head bobbing forward, the delayed sense that someone had struck her. Chiang rolled off the bleeding man to find a young boy standing over her, a white boy, maybe her age. He held the broken end of a bat in his trembling hands.

Chiang lunged forward. She watched as her arms tangled around the boy's legs, his eyes opening in horror. The boy brought the short piece of wood back down on her head, mimicking his father. It bounced off her head and out of his hands. He shrieked as Chiang wrapped herself around his knees and toppled him. She pulled herself up his frail body, hands grabbing fistfuls of his rumpled and smelly clothes, blood spilling out of her mouth and down her chin, mouthfuls of blood from the neck of the boy's father.

This boy's father, Chiang thought. *A boy.* She pulled herself toward his more youthful neck while his hands beat uselessly against her cheeks. She thought of Shen, the cute boy with the jet black hair who sat across from her at school. Chiang wondered suddenly if he had made it home that day. Was he out there, breaking into stores with his parents, killing animals like her with baseball bats?

The white boy screamed and begged. He was pleading with her. Sobbing. As if she had any choice.

Chiang opened her mouth. The boy's hands were on her face, covering her eyes, trying to push her away. He felt so thin. Like bones. Like a disappointing catch her father might curse as he cleaned for the salvageable scraps.

"No!" the boy screamed. His mother had fallen still. Chiang thought of all the flesh in the room. Weeks and weeks worth of flesh. The taste of the father was powerful on her lips.

She bent her head toward the boy's screaming throat and fought through his pushing and shoving arms, and she hated herself for this. It wasn't what she wanted, killing this boy who reminded her of Shen. But try as she might, Chiang couldn't do anything else. Even though she wanted to pull away, her head continued to bend toward his neck. She could add her own silent pleas to his, and yet her body moved to sate its hunger.

And Chiang was afraid. Not of these people, no longer, but of herself.

She wailed inside her own head. She yanked with her mind like a person inside one of those jackets from the movies, with the long arms strapped around the back, the crazy people. She bucked and jerked with her mind, tugging and pulling her head away, even as clacking teeth drew closer.

The boy was sobbing, crying, begging, digging his fingers at her eyes.

Chiang thought of the hours she had wrestled with a paintbrush, the long days with her tiny hands wrapped around the infuriating neck of her violin, practicing, practicing, perfecting. *Concentrate*, her mother would say. *Try harder*, her father would say.

Chiang concentrated. She tried harder than she'd ever tried concentrating on anything. The setting sun bounced through the streets and cast shadows across the spilled cans and the scene of violence. There was a symbol for *life* painted out there, but it read *stranger* from the inside. Chiang's lips brushed against the boy's throbbing neck. His poor arms were too weak. His mother stirred; Chiang could hear the lady's groans.

And then some handhold was reached. Like the thrill of her fingers finally bending into place and a sonorous and rewarding cry spilling from her violin—or the graceful arc of ink left from the supple perfection of her spinning wrist—there was this moment of complete control, this eyeblink of a mind taking over a body and bending raw impulse to graceful will.

Chiang's mouth brushed against the boy's neck, but she did not bite him there. She pulled away. *Really pulled away.* In charge for a slender moment.

When his hands came back to her face, pushing her, Chiang turned to the side and bit his finger. She crunched through to the bone and then bit down even harder. Her teeth went through the knuckle, the pop of something solid in her mouth, something to chew on as she fell away from the boy, a fleshy coating and a hard candy center.

The mother was stirring, holding her wounded side, coming to. The boy gasped and peered wide-eyed at his hand, clutching the spurting wound where his finger once stood. He would survive. Chiang knew very well that he would survive. She scrambled across the floor after the woman, still hungry, knowing what she needed to do. She glanced down at her hands as they brushed canned goods aside, at her missing fingers, the black char of her infected wound wrapping up her arm like a twisted tattoo, and Chiang was happy.

Look at what these people had brought her, she thought, as she turned the woman's groans into screams. Food and a way out. Flesh and blood. But more than that, as she bit the woman beneath the ear—

Company.

A friend.

Chiang ate and ate while the frightened boy beat her weakly and pathetically with what remained of his father's bat. She ate and smiled while his tormented screams filled her parents' shop. He was frightened, now, just as she had been. But that would change, Chiang thought to herself.

Everything does.

22 ❖ Dennis Newland

Lisa's face was a mess. Her chest had stopped heaving—the foamy bubbles of blood no longer gathering at the holes in her neck—and Dennis couldn't tell if there was enough of her left to come back or not. He'd seen others so eaten up that they didn't turn, just stayed dead.

He felt less horror than he thought he should over what he'd done. His body still tingled from the feed, from the raw fury of it all. But it was something else that kept him from being as frightened as he should have. It was over. The fucking dread was gone, the running and running, the fear. Over. He was what he was, and he could still think. He was still him. How long would that last?

Footsteps. Someone yelling his name. Lisa's name.

Neither of them said a thing.

Dennis left her where she lay and lumbered down the aisle of canned goods. It was hard to tell if he was in control. His body moved, and he seemed to go along with it. Confusing. Like a dream. A nightmare had ended, and now he was in a dream. He couldn't die. Nothing bad could happen to him. Dennis felt a thrill of immortality, of eating like he just ate, of reveling in the very thing he had spent weeks fearing.

Sneakers chirped as they approached aisle eighteen. Matt hurried around the corner, breathless, panting, shotgun in his hands. He stopped and gaped at the mess, the scattered cans, the spreading slick of blood. His eyes darted to Lisa on the ground and then to Dennis.

Dennis was nearly upon him, willing his legs faster, his gut gloriously and nauseatingly full. He'd seen the bloated ones among the crowds before, blood caked down their chins, and now he knew. He reached for his best friend, eager to end his running days as well. Just a bite, no room in his belly for a feed, and they would live forever, the both of them, immortal.

A roar. A skull-splitting bang. The furious bark of Matt's shotgun, and Dennis's leg was kicked out from underneath him, his thigh on fire, his ears ringing. He flopped forward, fingers brushing against Matt, face slamming into the floor, hands groping for his sneakers.

"Holy fuck, holy fuck, holy fuck..." Matt was saying.

Dennis clawed for his best friend, angry now. The fucker shot him. A groan leaked out, a mix of frustration and pain. As he crawled forward, he caught a glimpse of his own leg trailing behind, white bone and crimson muscle, his jeans and a good part of his thigh chewed off from the point-blank blast.

Fucker, I'm bringing you a gift, he wanted to say. This was it, the end of their running. It wasn't bad, wasn't death at all. It was just . . . *different*.

There was a clack as Matt pumped the gun, jacking another shell into the barrel. "No, no, no, no," his friend was saying, as if it were *his* head being aimed at, someone else's finger on the trigger, like he was the one who should be pissed.

More slaps of footfalls. A shriek. Dennis managed to get to his knees, what was left of one of them. He felt so full and happy. Matt was fucking it up. Sarah was screaming like they were back to day one, like she'd never seen anything like this before in her life.

Matt's shotgun was lowered at his face. Dennis tried to call out, to beg his friend to wait, the words a bloody hiss. As much as he wanted to duck and weave, to bob his head out of the way, all his body did was lumber forward, dragging a leg behind him, hands waving at the air as Matt took steps backwards.

"Fucking do it!" Sarah screamed. Tears coursed down her cheeks. Her eyes darted frantically from what was left of her friend to the mess Dennis had become. Dennis tried to beg Matt to swing the gun around on her. Couldn't he see? This was the end of things. This was the inevitable. The shotgun's long barrel shook, that cylinder of deep shadow aimed right between Dennis's eyes, the panic and terror rising up that his friend would do it, just as they had promised to each other all those long days ago.

"I'm sorry," Matt said. He was crying, too. His fucking best friend in the world, his new friend, his only friend, was crying. The shock was wearing off. Matt's jaw was set, old promises remembered. Sarah begged him, her hands on his arm, barrel trembling, and Dennis begged him as well in mute gurgles. A new fear took hold. This was the end, one pull of the trigger. For weeks, the terror of being turned had spurred them on, but it wasn't the fear of death, of not existing, but of existing like *this*. And now Dennis knew it wasn't that bad. There was nothing to be scared of. Except now, he was scared of his friend, of that barrel of deep shadow.

His screams filled his own head as he waited for it to come. Screams that tickled the region of his brain that could listen to silence, that could hear his own thoughts, the area where reading and nightmares took place. His fingertips brushed Matt's thigh, dragging one leg along, lurching forward.

"I'm sorry," Matt said again.

Set teeth. An ungodly thunderclap, a violence of noise, a trill of panic as Dennis braced for the end of all things.

He felt the blow to his other leg, felt it kick back behind him, the flesh flayed off by the eruption of metal pellets. Dennis flopped to the ground, utterly deaf, the world spinning and ringing, hot lava spreading from his knee to his groin.

For all his gyrations, he was able merely to roll over. One of his legs mostly didn't. It was attached by a few strands of soft tissue, skin and tendon and blue jean.

He heard Sarah's voice first, the high-pitched bitching joining the scream of sirens in his stunned eardrums. She was screaming Lisa's name, begging her boyfriend to do it, what had to be done.

And then Matt's voice, the deafness receding a notch, saying he couldn't, forgetting his promises, the pact they'd made. Saying, *goddammit* and *shut up, he fucking couldn't*.

Dennis lay there, his legs burning, his body on fire, arms waving at the air. Sarah ran past, blubbering, to cradle Lisa. Matt yelled at her to stay away. To stay the fuck away. He cocked the shotgun, the hollow *clunk* of an empty shell bouncing on the tile, and went to pull her off.

The two of them were cussing and crying as they hurried from the scene of what Dennis had done. They left him there, arms gyrating at the darkened ceiling, the smell of Lisa fading, a wheel on a shopping cart crying out as it was pushed along under a heavy load, and then silence. And a thought. A sickening thought for Dennis that this was how his forever would remain.

23 ❖ Chiang Xian

The throngs of sick tourists had wandered off, the streets outside full of the silent traffic of darting candy bar wrappers and the haze of smoke from unseen fires. There were pink smears on the glass, streaks of gore and abraded flesh where the undead had bumped and pressed and waved their stupid arms to get at the foul meat.

Chiang cared less and less for what went on out there. She had company, now. And while this boy—whose name would be Shen, she'd decided—stumbled and bumped in staggering circuits throughout the shop, she practiced chasing him, practiced controlling her feet, making a game of it, stopping now and then to eat from his parents before they lost their taste.

Shen, of course, hadn't quite the hang of it. He knocked things over and stumbled on the cans scattered about. He crawled up in the window display and sampled some of the rancid meat, even gnawed on her parents' shins. And since neither of them could talk, not yet at least, it was up to Chiang to supply the dialogue. She would crouch by Shen's father while the boy ate what was left of the man's thigh, and do both their voices over his loud smacking. Mostly, she would coach him, urging him to exert more will, to maybe one day help her move the heavy shelf blocking the door so they could both get out.

Practice, she would tell him, kicking a can, just an extra jerk of her knee as she was stepping along. *See? See?* she would shout. *I can do it, and so can you!*

The words would tumble out different, of course, like screams in a nightmare, but she thought it was getting better, that her tongue was learning just as her fingers and hands once had. Everyone has different abilities, she reminded herself. It was important to be patient with him. Some people had a hard time getting out of bed, forcing themselves to go to school. Some could just do it, always could. Different abilities. She would be patient.

In the meantime, she had a playmate to bump after in the meat shop. And so the two of them played chase during the day and a game she called *There-You-Are* at night. They played while the smell of their dead parents mingled in the air, and it was easy to pretend, if you knew how, that their grunts were giggles, their labored hisses the noise of happy laughter, just two kids wasting time while they wasted away, the both of them eying that heavy shelf by the door that kept them trapped inside.

Part III ✦ Jeffery Biggers

24 ❖ Jeffery Biggers

Where were the people? It was hard to figure at first, why with the outbreak there weren't more people. Ten million in New York, and most of them were just ... *gone.* Jeffery had assumed it would spread, that the avenues and streets would be crowded from one side to the other with the chompers. But then, most people didn't get away, did they? They got more than a bite. They got *consumed.*

And so the streets were full of cars, but no people. Just remains. That was the sickest thing, seeing the bones, all the cleaned carcasses. Getting bit and surviving was rarer than getting eaten whole. Rarer and worse. Being infected was hella worse. But so few got infected, right? How many got a scratch or a bite like Jeffery did and still managed to get clear, find a place to hole up until it weren't their choice how to move or what to do? Not many, he didn't figure. Most got eaten. That's where the ten million went. Gone. Eaten up and shat out by those who remained.

Jeffery remembered the one that got him. Goddamn that woman. Goddamn that crazy bitch.

He couldn't stop thinking about her, couldn't stop playing that day over and over in his head as he rode among the pack, weaving around the jammed cars with blinking hazards and open doors, a picked-clean skeleton sitting there in one of 'em with its seatbelt still on like it might crank the engine and go for a drive, some ad for a damn MADD commercial.

Jeffery remembered spotting the bitch from that upstairs apartment he'd staked out for his own. He hadn't planned on leaving that place until the cupboards were bare. Earlier that morning, he had escaped a few mobs, had used that combination of boot camp army know-how and the black spirit that had helped generations of his color make it through the deep shit time and time again. He'd seen some brutal stuff in his weeks of running, more gruesome even than the crap he'd seen in the war. Roadside bombs and flesh eaters had some things in common, except these monsters didn't leave limbs behind. They took them with them, munching on them like turkey legs while they tracked down another scent.

Jeffery had been surviving okay for a week or two, getting clear, avoiding one nick after another. Some of his friends weren't so lucky. Jeffery was used to that, the inequitable luck of two people sitting side-by-side in the same Hummer. One man gets a scratch, the other is holding his guts in his lap and screamin' for his momma. All luck. Where you're sittin', where you're born. Dumb fucking luck.

Well, there's dumb luck, and then there's just plain stupid. Jeffery had been stupid, trying to save that baby, thinking shit could be saved anymore. Stupid.

He'd seen the woman from the apartment window, down in the alley, three stories below. One of the flesh-eaters was walking in circles, waving her arms over her head. Hadn't seen one do that. Most walked with their arms out like goddamn Frankenstein, like the soul trapped inside can see but the shit in charge can't. Like they gotta feel their way through the breeze.

So this one, arms wiggling like thick snakes over her head and around her shoulders, spinning and spinning all alone. He figured what the fuck? What's her disorder? Jeffery had watched from the window, curious, eating someone else's potato chips, whoever the fuck used to live there. And then he saw what the damn flesh-eating bitch was doing. Naw, he *heard* it. It was the wail of the living—a baby awake, screaming from one of those goddamn yuppie backpacks. The mother must've just turned in the last day or two for that thing to still be alive. Jeffery leaned out the window to see better. Damn woman was waving her arms, trying to get at the morsel of noisy flesh strapped to her back, trying to eat her own goddamn baby.

Up till then, Jeffery had done well by looking out for himself—no point risking *two* lives where one was in jeopardy. Hell, he'd seen so many dead by that point, so many go down that could've been him if he were a little slower, if he'd hesitated or panicked, if he'd stuck his neck out for someone else.

But something about the baby's cries got to him. That sound dove into his bones and clawed at something deep, something primal. Maybe it was this last chance at life. All the death and dying, and here was something that'd just been born, a memory of how shit used to work. The thought of leaving that baby to starve to death on its mother's back—or worse, for those writhing arms to finally get it free, for those clacking teeth to set to work—he couldn't sit there and wait.

He remembered leaning out the window and scanning the alley. There was a van crashed into the corner of the building, the hood buckled up around the old brick. The body of the van blocked the alley off from the street. It looked safe enough. Boxed in. One woman spinning in circles, grunting and groaning. Jeffery set the bag of chips aside, wiped the grease off on his blue jeans, and threw his leg out the window. After a moment's hesitation, he scrambled onto the fire escape.

A gas grill blocked access to the ladder—a ghetto balcony. Pots of dirt with wilted brown stalks lay over on their sides, a luckier kind of dead. Jeffery wrestled the grill out of the way, metal squealing on metal. He flashed a glance across the alley at a spot of movement, saw a young man watching him from a window in the building over, late teens or early twenties. Surviving age, as Jeffery had come to think of it. The boy leaned out the window and looked down at the woman in the alley. Jeffery squeezed around the grill and descended the metal stairs.

At the end of the stairs, he knelt and started to free the telescoping ladder at the bottom, but wondered if the chompers could manage to scramble up. He was pretty sure they couldn't, but why risk it, now that he'd found someplace safe? He gauged the distance below and figured he could jump up and grab the lowest rung, used to go around the neighborhood leaping up and doing pull-ups on 'em to impress his friends when he was younger. Better safe than sorry, so he left the ladder the way it was.

He scrambled down the rungs, the cries from the baby louder now and somehow soothing. The noise it made was a sign that it was still alive, that the woman hadn't gotten it free. Jeffery didn't know what he'd do to take care of the thing. Maybe it'd be his ticket onto one of the rescue helicopters he'd heard about but had never seen. If they were real, the baby would be his way on board. Jeffery could be that soldier helping a friend cradle his guts for a change. He remembered. They always took that other soldier out of the shit-storm. They saw him helping like that, squeezing a friend's grave wound, and they treated him like some necessary bandage, some emotional tourniquet. Jeffery would save the baby and be saved himself. That became the plan.

Working down to the last rung, he dangled there for a moment, feet swinging high over the windswept garbage in the alley, the grunts from the woman changing as she spotted him there, as she caught his scent.

Jeffery let go and dropped through the air to the pavement. He landed in a crouch, moving from a safe world to one of danger, a slender bridge having been crazily crossed.

The woman staggered toward him, hands opening and closing like a crab's pinchers. Jeffery hadn't thought this through. He scrambled backwards, feet kicking through loose newspaper and swollen bags of trash chewed open by rats.

The lady moved like a drunk. Jeffery's heart pounded through his sweatshirt. He thought he heard the whistle of mortars whizzing down toward his base in the middle of the night, that feeling that death was everywhere and it could suddenly choose *you*. But this weren't mortars. He could see her coming. Could outrun her. He told himself there weren't nothin' to be afraid of.

Hurrying backwards, Jeffery made some space between him and her. One thing about the chompers was that they never stopped. Always coming forward, lips flapping, eyes unblinking, arms out. They were fuckin' tireless. He grabbed a lid off one of the metal trashcans. The baby had fallen quiet. The damn thing had better make it, risking his neck like this. An aluminum painter's pole rested against the pipes that ran up the side of the building, a crusted roller still on the end. He grabbed it as well and glanced up at the boy watching from the window, wondering how crazy he looked down in that alley with a lid and a stick, a shield and a sword.

The woman in the dress kept coming. Jeffery waited, a tight grip on the lid's handle, the dented metal resting against his forearm, the pole in his other hand. She was nearly within reach when he finally spotted the wound that'd turned her. It was at the base of her neck, a nasty bite, the gurgles and moans leaking from there rather than her lips. The dried blood running down her neck and chest was like a red scarf tucked into her dress. Her crab-claws pinched for him. Jeffery swung his shield and knocked her arms aside. The woman did a pirouette, bending at the waist as she flailed for balance. He lunged forward and shoved her in the back, tried to get his feet tangled in hers, but in a drunken stagger she shuffled out of the way. He tried again, the baby watching him with wide, white eyes, and this time the bitch flopped forward into the garbage.

Jeffery was on her before she could push her way to her feet. He kept a knee at the base of her spine, easy as pie, dropped the pole and the lid and fumbled with the clasps on the pack. He should have brought a knife from the kitchen to cut the damn thing free. The woman's arms slid back and forth through the trash, the rotten fruit rinds, the empty tin cans, like it was tryin' to make a snow angel. An alley angel, Jeffery thought to himself. He was giddy. Laughing. The adrenaline was melting away, the fear fading to a tingling sense of relief now that she was pinned on her belly, jaws well away from him. It reminded Jeffery of the sound of a distant mortar blast, knowing a tent down the row had caught the whistling reaper and not you. He worked one buckle loose and moved to the other. The baby's little arms twirled in mimicry of its mother's, little pink lips kissing the air, mother and son both hungry and grunting and crying from being so close to each other, so close to the sustenance they needed, neither of them able to reach it.

The other buckle finally came free. Jeffery yanked the straps out from under the pinned and writhing woman.

He slid his knee up her spine to where the baby had been, listened to her teeth clack shut over and over, head turned to the side, eyes straining for a sight of him, eager to eat them both.

The baby cried. Jeffery took his time strapping the kid to his back, made sure the buckles were tight. He eyed the jump down the alley, thinkin' how heavy the kid was, if he could still make the leap. Hadn't thought this shit through. Not at all.

The boy in the window above whistled at him. Jeffery glanced up and frowned at the kid for all his waving and shouting. Stupid fool, making all that noise, gonna summon more of 'em.

And then Jeffery saw where the kid was pointing. He looked toward the van, cold fear clawing at his guts, as Jeffery Biggers saw that the boxed-in alley weren't so empty anymore.

25 ❖ Jeffery Biggers

Jeffery could still hear that baby's wails. He could feel the little guy writhing against his back, legs kicking, lungs screaming, missing his mother. But the baby and his mother were long gone. And as he stumbled along the Hudson through cleaned bones and past skeletons jumbled and missing pieces, he flashed back to that mother pinned beneath his knee, face down in alley filth, swimming through that accumulation of garbage like she was tryin' to get somewhere.

"Fuck," he remembered saying, realizing his situation. He remembered the bark of a cuss, a war-born habit. And even though the shit of the world had been up to his eyeballs in that closed-in alley, some part of him had felt bad for droppin' the F-bomb around the kid. As if the tyke were even old enough to learn words. As if a word were any worse a thing to learn than all the craziness beneath Jeffery's knee and crowding past that wrecked van. Words were hollow compared to this, and yet some of them still felt good to say. Good and wrong, what with that kid strapped to his back.

There were six or seven of the air-chomping assholes in the alley. They squeezed between the wrecked van's rear bumper and the brick apartment building, drawn in by the baby's screams, no doubt. There was a loud pop at Jeffery's feet. He glanced up, thinking something had been dropped from above, then felt a thing brush up against his boot. Flinching, he slapped his hand at the trash to shoo off the rats and felt the mother's hand grabbing for him, instead.

Glancing down, Jeffery saw her arm snaking back around at him, out of joint, muscles so desperate to get at him that they'd popped her shoulder. He gagged at the sight, this misshapen animal face-down in open bags of rotten garbage, an arm waving at him like some appendage, like a tentacle or tail. What the fuck was he doing down there? And the baby's screams were deafening—it was fucking up his mojo. What they hell had he been thinkin', dropping into that alley? He'd been munching potato chips five minutes ago, safe and sound, and now this.

The half dozen chompers reached the dangling fire escape. Too many to dodge. Jeffery wasn't sure if he could make the bottom rung in one try, anyway, not with the baby on his back. While the chompers shuffled toward him, he scanned the alley, his heart pounding, for sure they'd gotten him now. Him and the baby. Fucking pointless, coming down there, trying to save anything in that world.

Behind him, the opposite end of the alley ended abruptly in a brick wall. A building had been planted between two other buildings, New York's empty alleys serving as vacant lots. The chompers were twenty paces away, and Jeffery had to move. He had to release the pissed off mom beneath his knee, needed to make a run for it. He cursed the developers who'd clogged the alleys with their skinny-ass buildings, who'd bricked up so many windows, who'd made runnin' and survivin' an absolute bitch.

There was a dumpster across the way. Jeffery made sure the yuppie backpack thing was snug over his shoulders. He grabbed the aluminum pole he'd dropped in the trash, looked for the trashcan lid, decided to leave it, and dashed to the large green container. His knees banged on the metal as he scampered up on the plastic lid. The thing rang hollow, its booming echoes upsetting the child and setting off its wails once more.

The dumpster's lid sagged under his weight. Jeffery glanced up to see the kid from earlier hanging out his window, watching him. Fucking spectator. Jeffery remembered watching his fair share of disasters the past weeks, wondering when he'd be on the other side. And now here he was. He gazed longingly over the heads of the scrambling groaners as they arrived at the dumpster and clawed and banged against it. The black painted ladder of the fire escape dangled from the sky, an apartment up there that he knew was clean, no chompers hiding in the bathroom, some food and diet cokes in the pantry.

The mother with the fucked-up shoulder righted herself and joined the others around the dumpster. A few were actually trying to climb up, were miming with their legs like walking up steps, the stupid fucks. Jeffery could smell them over his own weeks-old ripeness. A fucking mass grave, that's what they smelled like. He was standing over the lip of that one in Samawah, the reek of rotting flesh swirling up out of the desert soil. Goddamn, nothing smelled worse than the long dead. The mother waved one arm for her baby, wanting to eat the damn thing and Jeffery both. Its other arm hung like a flapping sleeve by its body, the shoulder not right. More of the chompers were squeezin' in between the van and the building. No fuckin' way out. Goddamn. And that mother really had her eyes set on him.

The lid to the dumpster popped and shifted beneath his feet. Jeffery backed up toward the brick wall behind him. No windows low down on this side of the alley. He pushed against the building to see if he could slide the dumpster on its rusted wheels. No fuckin' way. Like trying to shove a Hummer uphill. The goddamn undead were rustlin' the thing, though. The dumpster was shakin' and jivin' as they bumped mindlessly for the meat up on the lid.

Fuckin' meat. All those chompers wanted was a bite of his flesh. At least, if he went like this, he'd be a pile of bones. Better that than a nick and getting free. He'd seen both cases. Better to be bones.

The baby stopped screaming. It left the alley full of the grunts and ahhs from the hungry dead. Their teeth clacked on the air, their empty and unblinking eyes fixated on Jeffery. And oh, fuck, he had this idea. Fuck. He glanced up the wall and saw the kid in the window still peepin' at his misadventures, leaning out over the sill. Black boy. Local, probably. In his teens, younger than Jeffery had figured at first. Goddamn, it'd suck to have anyone watch this. Like a fuckin' conscience. Like God himself staring down while you did something gravely wrong.

Jeffery thought of all the times he'd been too terrified to masturbate when he was that boy's age, worried God was watching. Now he worried about this teenager seeing what he was about to do. He loosened the yuppie pack. The chompers wanted meat. Jeffery had meat on him.

The baby resumed its wailing as soon as he got it free. It wailed as he held it out, dangling it like a bag of takeout over the undead, and this awful idea formed solid like a scab in Jeffery's mind.

Starving eyes lifted to the baby. The dumpster jostled as the damn thing was surrounded, arms waving, more chompers crowding in, nudging the large metal box with their gyrations and hungry growls.

Jeffery felt the eyes from above, staring down. Goddamn, he thought. Don't watch this shit. He held the aluminum painter's pole between his knees and loosened the plastic rings that let the sections extend, let the brush reach those high ceilings. *Please, God*, Jeffery thought. *Please don't watch this shit—*

26 ❖ Jeffery Biggers

Days had passed since he'd dropped down into that alley, and Jeffery had run the end of his life over and over in his mind. There was always something he'd change, a knife to take down with him, lowering that damn ladder, being just a bit faster, but never a regret about going in general. Never a pang of regret for that child.

He headed south. There was no traffic—the noise of the city had just stopped, those great and ceaseless rivers of mostly yellow falling perfectly still. The last bit of flow had come days ago with that white pickup that'd barreled through Harlem, an old man behind the wheel trying his damnedest to get the fuck out. He had plowed through row after row of chompers like high corn, tossing bodies aside and running them over.

When his front axle got stuck on a pile of crushed chompers—mounds of them like deep mud—the man had tried rocking it back and forth, the transmission growling as he threw it in and out of gear. Gathering around him, the starving mob had banged on the glass while spinning rubber tore through the bodies stuck beneath the cab. Arms had waved under there like thick grass, the rest of the person crushed. And the smell, an odor horrible enough to drown out all the other horrible smells, rubber and flesh both heating up to burning.

Jeffery hadn't been one of the lucky ones that got run over, hadn't been one of those too far away to miss out on the feed. He'd been somewhere in the middle, that worst place possible.

That had been the last time he'd seen a moving vehicle, that white man in that white truck plowing through the hordes of chompers. Now the streets stood still, grotesque and disfigured men and women prowling among the cars like bugs picking through rocks. High above, shapes moved behind shimmering windows, no telling if the people inside were dead or undead, not unless there was a jagged hole and the breeze blew just the right way.

This was what his city had become. Shattered glass, unmoving traffic, hungry packs roaming aimlessly.

But not Jeffery. He was aimless no longer. He felt a pull southward like the slope of a crater, felt drawn by more than the mere scent of the living. Drawn by something else.

It occurred to him, as he strode toward the winter sun in its low, noonday position, that this wasn't the first time he had looked south while all the traffic stopped. He had been fourteen when the planes hit. He remembered the smell, that acrid odor of asbestos and melted steel and who knew what else. Paper had fluttered on the breeze clear up to Harlem, little charred pieces of the stuff like burning snow. That was how white-collar buildings bled: They leaked paperwork, filing cabinets full of the shit, coughing it out through broken glass to flap in the same wind that brought the smoke all the way up to Harlem.

The wind had been out of the south that day, just like it was right then. It was the world's way of sharing its misery with the whole island, the stench flowing through the glass caverns of uptown, over the park, and infecting the colored streets with the ruin of a white man's world.

At the time, of course, Jeffery hadn't known what the smoke was all about, hadn't understood the sickness at the yoke of those planes, but he knew a personal attack when he saw one. He knew when a man fronted you, you didn't back down. Men were like dogs. You give 'em something to chase, and they'll chase it. You turn, and they'll bite you.

And so his mother had cried when he'd enlisted. Jeffery didn't tell her beforehand. Shit, she still had the acceptance letter from Medgar Evers on the fridge when he deployed, dreamed of him coming home and getting a business degree, dreamed of him coming home at all.

Jeffery told everyone it was 9/11 that made him sign up. Part of him believed it. The rest of him knew better. He had known since he was born that he would go off and fight in a war, whether he wanted to or not. His old man had fought. Back in his father's day you were drafted by law rather than circumstance. The world sent a man off to fight another man who had never fronted at all, just wanted to be left alone. It weren't like Pearl Harbor or 9/11, some slap in the face like that shit. His old man said it was just confused men killing confused men so they might be the one to come home in one piece. That was all.

Jeffery believed him. He knew his father. Not like *knew-who-he-was,* but really knew him. That bullshit about black boys not knowing who their daddies were drove him fucking crazy. Every kid he grew up with knew who his daddy was. How could you not, when your momma spent most of her days cursing his name over and over, telling her kids what a shit that man was. Most everyone knew their father, sometimes got a letter or a guilty glance on the street, but Jeffery was different. He *knew* his dad. They'd spent hours and hours bullshitting after the war, drinking malts on the stoop while kids screamed down the street and traffic drifted by, his father telling him the shit he'd seen, Jeffery keeping mostly quiet.

The talks would last until nine o'clock, when his dad would get up, knees making noises, and reach out a hand calloused from handling ropes all day. The Liberty Landing Ferry made its first run at five in the morning. Jeffery's dad had to be on the boat by four-thirty. So they would shake hands around nine, father and son, and his dad would glance up at the lit window a few stories above but never ask how she was doing.

"No one told you that you *had* to do it," his father often said back then, referring to the fighting Jeffery had done.

And Jeffery had known right from the start what his old man was trying to say. There was something different about volunteering, something else about being *taken*. All the questions about who he was dating, was he in love, what's she like, any kids? Jeffery knew his old man. He had worried that his son, this second chance at life, a life full of freedom and free of mistakes, would mess up and lose the same wars he'd lost. The same wars overseas and battles in those streets. Battles in one's own mind.

But Jeffery couldn't lose. That only happened when a man fronted you, when you turned and ran. Wars were only lost when they breathed down your neck. And so Jeffery headed south, drawn by more than the breeze, freer in some ways than the unthinking monsters crushing and bumping all around him, pulled down the slope of that distant crater, and not for the first time.

There was something else the same, he saw. It was the crowds, just like all those years ago. People had staggering about, confused, dazed, half-dead. Jeffery didn't know what the smoke meant back then, but he knew where his dad worked. Something bad had happened on the tip of the island.

He was cutting class that day, not because he did it often, but the weather had been too nice for being inside. He could feel it that morning when he left the apartment, the crispness in the air like a spring or fall day that would warm up to something special. The sort of day where clouds played hooky, and so should he.

At first, people said it was a bomb. Some said it was a fire or a small plane, like a Cessna. All Jeffery knew was that it had happened at the World Trade Center, and that's where his father worked. That's where he said he worked, anyway. Jeffery had never been. All the weekends he'd been invited out to ride the boat back and forth across the Hudson, and he'd never been.

He went that time, on that day many years ago, but not by choice. His young legs just took him at a trot, his thoughts rattling around in his skull, people on the sidewalks acting crazy, the traffic coming to a halt.

Some others had moved with him, more and more, curiosity flowing south. He remembered angling toward the river, noticing the change in the traffic, the cars backed up at the tunnel, a sudden explosion in cops and firefighters. They yelled at him and others to turn around, more cops than he'd ever seen.

The blocks had gone by in a blur. He remembered his father arriving at their apartment once, smiling and sweating, claiming to have walked all the way there from work. Jeffery didn't believe him. No one walked the length of the island. But jogging it that day, gray smoke clogging a cloudless sky, blocks and blocks drifting by of stuck traffic and people holding their phones, mouths covered with trembling hands, Jeffery saw that the island weren't as big as he liked to think.

He never got there, of course, to where the smoke was coming from. The crowds heading south bumped into the much different crowds fleeing north. This is what reminded him of that day eleven years ago, what looked the same between the island getting hit and bit. The people staggering north back then had been pale, skin white like ghosts, even the brothers and sisters. They looked like the dead, their eyes these dark and unblinking circles. They pawed at their own faces, groaning, holding shoulders to see where they were going, just like the undead did now.

Jeffery remembered how they cried and moaned, how they fell in the streets, shaking. People were hugging whoever was there, was closest, didn't matter. Jeffery remembered that. It didn't matter.

A cop had told him to get lost. He picked Jeffery out of the downtown crowd, could tell that he was different, didn't belong. Jeffery's skin glistened with sweat from the long run, his eyes wide with curiosity, wide with all he hadn't seen. They were different than the look from those who *had*.

"My daddy's down there," he tried to tell the cop.

"Then your dad's in a world of hurt," the officer had said.

Jeffery had been pissed. It was a shitty thing to say. But he realized later that the cop was just like him. There was no blanket of ash on that man, no desire to hug a stranger. He hadn't seen. Hadn't seen a thing. Was just reacting. Drafted into a war, not asked.

His father, Jeffery would learn, was not in a world of hurt. He was helping that world. The ferry had run back and forth across those cold September waters for much of the morning, people piling aboard from the seawall like an army of the undead, more and more of them, always coming, crowding aboard pale as ghosts and shaking like grocery bags caught on a clothesline. And Jeffery's dad, hands rough from handling ropes all those long years, had been there, pulling those people aboard.

27 ❖ Jeffery Biggers

The dumpster lurched as the dead knocked against it, and Jeffery nearly fell on his ass. He steadied himself and held the extended aluminum pole with both hands, leaving him with only his jutting elbows for balance. More bangs, and the dumpster slid a few inches, tired wheels groaning, the hollow metal resounding beneath him.

It was working. Holy shit, it was working!

Jeffery spread his feet, his knuckles pale as he gripped that cool aluminum pole, his arms shaking from the strain of holding the thing out as far as he could.

They'd done this in boot camp, he remembered. It was a form of punishment. Made them hold their rifles by the barrels, parallel to the ground, the heavy butts dipping toward the earth. Joints and muscles would scream while the drill sergeant came around and rested his pasty hands on the stocks, pressing them down.

The dumpster moved again. The baby wailed. Beneath it, dozens of hands pawed at the air like drunken fans at a concert, like kids lining a parade, hoping for someone on a float to throw them candy.

The thing they craved swung from one of those yuppie backpacks. It was looped over the crusty paint roller, the pole bending under the strain. The alley had collected a mob. Some stood waving beneath the kid. Others crowded from the far side—and the dumpster shifted.

Jeffery laughed and shuffled his feet on the unsteady plastic lid. It was fucking working. If he got out of this shit, he'd have a helluva story for the next group he bumped into. He was already retelling it as the dumpster moved a few more inches, the casters squealing as they worked free. The body of the metal container rang with the angry bangs of scrambling arms and legs trying to get up from the other side. The ones on the near side weren't trying to climb at all, just fixating on the little feet wheeling in the air over their heads. One crowd pushed and the other did nothin', and the dumpster moved.

A hand got close to the screaming kid, a tall fucker. Jeffery bit his lip and steadied the pole. Goddamn, this was wrong. But it weren't like he was throwing the kid over their heads and making a dash. Hell, he didn't have to risk his neck to be down there in the first place.

The dumpster moved quite a bit, the kid swinging in its harness, Jeffery letting go with one hand and swinging his free arm for balance. He used the kid like bait to guide some of the chompers between the dumpster and the brick wall behind him. They followed like sheep. As they crowded in and scrambled for the prize, the dumpster really moved.

It lurched away from the building, and more of them filed into place. Too damn easy. Too predictable.

He swung the kid around and steered the biggest crush of foul undead toward the other side of the alley, getting the hang of it. There was an urge to glance up at his audience above, the boy in the window, to shout out that he was gonna be okay, but there was so much to concentrate on. He switched hands and gave his other one a shake, fingers tingling. The plastic lid buckled some more. Jeffery had a thought of falling through, of losing his platform. The paranoia that'd built up over weeks of running told him this would happen next. The worst shit possible would always happen next. And there would be a goddam chomper *in* the dumpster, lying in wait. He shook this thought away. That's not how this was going down. He was already telling the story to the next group, telling them how near he'd come from having his bones picked clean. He was gonna make it.

A few inches at a time, the dumpster crept across the alley. More of the fuckers squeezed in around the wrecked van, joining the pack. Jeffery worried it would be too many, that the crush would get so dense that the dumpster would simply stop moving. He was already out in the center of the alley, an island in a shark-infested sea. Man, this would be a story. He laughed with nerves, the metallic taste of adrenaline on his tongue, thinking of all the times he'd been shot at and how he thought it'd make for a good story back home. Fuck, he shoulda re-upped. Another tour, and he'd be safer over there than he was now.

One of the undead managed to get its armpits up on the lip of the dumpster, scrambling over some of those that'd fallen down. Jeffery kicked him in the head. He tried to keep toward the edges of the lid where it was more solid, but hands were brushing his boots. Shit, this was tenuous. Tightroping this motherfucker. Six feet away from the nearest window. Four feet. Almost three feet, when his plan hit a snag. The bastards on that side of the dumpster wouldn't clear out. They were like a bumper, a wall, blocking progress.

He shifted hands again and tried urging them out with the kicking and screaming kid, but more took their place from the other side. Jeffery was fucked. He looked back at the kid in the window, needing to see some other living soul, and the boy's wide eyes and slack mouth confirmed his own fears: well and truly fucked.

He pulled the kid back in. The chompers were piling up, banging into the dumpster from all sides. Soon they would start forming ramps and making their way to the top. Jeffery pictured them crashing through the lid with him, banging on the insides of the reeking container, being eaten away at from all sides, him and the baby, mixing in the same guts.

Fuck. Fuck.

He loosened the backpack from the end of the painting handle and worked his arms through the straps. "C'mon, kid," he breathed. The groans and the stench were everywhere. This was it. This was it. He twisted the knobs on the handle again and extended it all the way, really cinched them down tight. Another fucker was up to her armpits, face caked in blood, a real hungry one. Jeffery stepped away and concentrated on the window. "C'mon, kid." He speared the glass with the handle, punching it through panes set in place in the 50s, maybe earlier. Several more pokes and the window was busted up good. He used the pole to slap the glass out of the frame—thank God they didn't have them damn bars on them—and kicked the bitch in the head who was biting after his boots. Fuck. Fuck. Chomper slobber on his goddamn boots.

The thin strips of wood that formed a grid between the panes of glass were all that was left. Like an empty game of tic-tac-toe. No breaking them with the painting stick, but how sturdy could they be? Jeffery pulled the stick back, used it to push a chomper's forehead away, the thing snarling angrily at being toyed with by its food. The plastic lid faintly buckled. The banging and groaning were like drums reaching some sort of crescendo. Even the kid had fallen quiet, maybe for being pressed back against a body, maybe just fuckin' exhausted, maybe sensing what Jeffery was sensing: that the end was well fucking nigh.

He ran along the edge of the lid to keep it from collapsing, ran past the waving and groping hands, trying not to trip over them, and threw himself through the void, over the heads, jumping like a kid again, back when he liked to pretend the ground was lava.

He crashed halfway through the wooden slats. They snapped by his shoulders and arms, his waist catching on the window, feet scrambling. An old wound on his stomach lanced out with a pain so sudden and sharp that he nearly fainted. It felt like one of the slats had fucking pierced him, but it was just a deep bruise that would never heal, a former injury being struck again.

Hands fell on his calves. One of his boots was torn off as he tried to pull himself inside, damn things screaming and moaning and his body on fire with a thousand aches.

Jeffery scrambled through the busted window, one boot on, another off. He laughed and whooped. He jumped around a disgusting living room torn up by scavengers, the baby hollering on his back, its voice going up and down as it rode the sickening roller coaster of Jeffery's elation.

With a loud hack and coughing noise, and then a splatter of nasty warmness against his neck, the kid lost the last meal it would ever get from its mother. Jeffery didn't give a shit. He laughed at this, knowing it was the perfect punch line to the goddamn most unbelievable bullshit story anyone in this living nightmare would ever share with another wide-eyed and doubting soul.

He limped around on his one boot, laughing. *Limping.* The aches wore off from holding that painting stick so far out, from smashing through the goddamn window. Limping. Looking down. Blood on the filthy carpet, blood on his sock.

"No," Jeffery muttered. "Oh, fuck, fuck, no." He hopped to the sofa with its stuffing erupting like pearly white guts.

"Fuck me, no. C'mon, kid. C'mon."

Jeffery sat down and tore off his sock, hand shaking. His bladder felt near to burst with diet coke. No. Not after all that. No fucking way.

The sock came away easy, the blood not nearly begun to set, not an old wound like he'd hoped, not a scab ripped open like he prayed it was.

"Oh, fuck, kid."

Jeffery worked at the buckles on the yuppie pack. He pulled the infant around and laid him gently on his back amid the disgorged white furniture innards. He had no idea how old the child was, always got that wrong whenever he guessed. It coulda been born yesterday. Could be three months. No fuckin' clue.

He studied the wound. Saw the bite marks, the torn flesh. Knives in the kitchen, probably. He could saw through the thing, hack through the bone. But he'd heard from that one group that it didn't work. They said their one-armed friend was still out there somewhere, clacking at the air with his teeth. It'd been no good at all to cut his arm off.

The kid looked at him with something like worry, with his little nose and raised brow. There were angry bangs and groans from the alley heard through the smashed window. The infant had those big eyes babies have, those little pink lips all puckered up, askin' for their next meal. Just like Jeffery and all the survivors, just like that alley full of chompers, everyone was always looking for their next meal.

Jeffery studied the little guy, the kid who was supposed to've been his ticket out of there. A one-way ride on one of them helicopters, always the helicopters coming to pull him out of the deep shit. Just one more ride, that's all he wanted. Come and get me. Save me from my own goddamn country. Here's the red smoke right fuckin' here. Here's me waving my rifle, barrel pointed right back at me, motherfuckers, just like you taught. Here I am. Come and get me.

Jeffery looked down at his foot, dripping blood.

They already had, he figured. They'd already got him fucking good.

28 ✤ Jeffery Biggers

Jeffery could still feel that original wound, but he no longer limped. He walked just as unsteadily on *both* legs. And what control he could exert over where they took him seemed to come from resignation. That's how he could somewhat operate his body. The less he struggled, the more say he had in where he went. He could steer by *thinking* about a place, by leaning into the walls of his own self—not aggressively, that didn't work—but just a gradual lean, like guiding a bowling ball after it had already left his hand. It reminded Jeffery of the Buddhists he'd read about, their fascination with water, how it flowed to fill any vessel, how it moved around a pier rather than put up a fight and try and bash through it.

It was one of his dad's books, a ratty paperback passed to him on the stoop, a book he'd never finished. His old man was always bringing him worn books with chipped edges and broken spines that smelled of wet rope and low tide. He said he read them while the ferry was waiting on passengers. Jeffery never asked where his father got the books, always assumed he stole them from those racks of dollar paperbacks crazy white bookstore owners left on the sidewalk like a temptation. He tended to assume the worst about his old man. It was hard not to, growing up in a nest with his momma's hate—all those vile thoughts regurgitated and forced down Jeffery's open beak.

Most of the books his father gave him went in the trash. He would try and read them, try and sell them, but they rarely took to him or were taken up by others. The only book his old man ever gave him that he read cover to cover was the one on sculpture. It was a guilty pleasure, that book. Not sure what the draw was, and Jeffery had never told anyone about it. His father had brought it one day to show Jeffery where he worked. There was a picture of two sculptures by the water, two towers. *The Pylons*, the book called them. They sat on the edge of the Hudson right there at the World Trade Center where his father's boat docked six times a day.

"A black man made these," his father had said.

The picture showed the two sculptures looking out over the river toward Jersey, a big clock on the other side that his father said all the men in suits could see clear across the Hudson so they could manage their time, clock in and clock out, cinch up or loosen their ties.

"This is where we been," his old man had said, tapping one of the towers. It was a blocky structure, the corners sharp and built of heavy stone. It had sections, like the body of an insect, six or seven of them. They got more squat toward the bottom, all of them pointing down into the earth. It was the saddest thing Jeffery had ever seen, this coming before he'd seen war. Something about the heavy weight of those sections, crushing each other, made it the most heartbreaking of sights.

It looked like the sculpture was being driven into the earth, the sections on top weighing the others down, the ones on the bottom squashed and flattened. And maybe those towers could represent anything a person wanted to see, but Jeffery saw what his old man saw. This was their race captured by a brother sculptor; this was the generations piling up on those that came before. Once you saw it like that, it was impossible to see anything else.

"And this is us dreamin'," his father said, running his finger across the neighboring tower. "This is hope."

If the stone sculpture made Jeffery frown without knowing why, if it made his gut sink, this one made him suck in his breath. It was a sculpture crafted of air. A wire frame, twisting and weaving, pointing up like smoke rising toward the sky. It was a sister's braids. It was a dozen long-fingered hands interlocked with glory, the blue sky caught between their palms. It was the flutter above a choir as those voices and arms and those gaping sleeves raised up and lost themselves in their own song.

A black man had made these, his father had told him. This was where he worked.

That chapter was about a man named Martin. Here were these two towers, sadness and joy, hope and resignation, side by side. It was a father on a stoop, back bent, the years driving him toward his grave. It was a son with a thrust chest and lifted chin, full of dreams and news of enlistment. It was a boy signing up for a thing he didn't know, vigor in his limbs, hopes and wishes of becoming a man in other men's eyes. It was a sculpture of the before and after, of that man returning home, cast out of a war he understood even less having looked it in its eyes, his belly a knot of scars from where they'd pulled out bits of Hummer, shoved him back together, sewn him up.

Jeffery felt the pull of those towers, that place, that zero ground, that wharf where his old man wrapped lines around bollards and greeted passengers while the captain stood on the deck smoking cigarettes. He felt the pull of those towers, a Pylon full of life pointing toward the heavens, one full of despair driving deep into the earth.

He had spent hours looking at that picture, but he had never seen them with his own eyes.

A block away, as he leaned south, guiding his limbs like water around a pier, he heard the sounds of a fight, the familiar pops of gunfire that used to mean grabbing your helmet and running off to kill someone. Sounds that now meant there were still people alive and able to put up a fight. Jeffery could smell living meat and fresh fear in the direction of the gunfire. Most of the tottering undead around him angled that way, picking up the pace, pushing deeper into the heart of the financial district.

But not Jeffery. He leaned on the walls of the hollow thing he'd become, this walking fist of hunger, this shell grown exhausted from not sleeping. He steered toward the unfinished skyscraper standing in the empty space where two other towers once stood, an incomplete boy trying to stand proud now that its parents were gone. He saw Winter Garden, a glass dome his father had described in whispers, these landmarks a simple walk from his home, but he had never taken the time to visit. All within reach, a long walk, that place where those towers stood, those Pylons near where his father worked, but he had never taken the time to visit. Not even back when he could.

29 ❖ Jeffery Biggers

Jeffery knew from watching unfortunate others that he didn't have long. Fifteen minutes? Twenty? He'd seen it go fast for neck bites. Seen it take almost an hour for that big brother who'd lost a finger and had asked to be locked down with bike chains. Decisions. Damn. He had run this shit through his mind every possible way a thousand times, but it was different now with the clock ticking, with the sickness spreading in his veins. Damn. Fifteen minutes to off himself or to crawl away somewhere safe where he wouldn't be eaten, where he could slip off into that gazing stupor people went into until they came back as something else.

Fifteen minutes. He gazed at the smashed window he'd come through. The frustrated gurgles and hungry groans could be heard from the alley. The dumpster was still being knocked around out there. One dive back through, he thought. Give them what they want, make sure there was nothing left. Go be bones.

The kid kicked his legs on the sofa beside him, riding an imaginary bike. Jeffery looked over and watched the boy yawn, eyes puckered shut, tiny hands waving at the air. No one would ever teach him how to ride a bike. That shit was through. This kid had no idea what he'd been born into. In fact, he looked bored, like: *let's get this over with, motherfucker.*

Jeffery looked around the apartment. No lurkers. Safe, not like that mattered. It was the typical wreck he'd seen the last weeks: cabinets standing open, drawers a-kilter, nothing put back in its place. The coffee table had been used as an ashtray. It smelled like the sink had been used as a toilet. The fucking world he lived in. *Used* to live in. How much longer?

The goddamn kid. Jeffery felt like his own father must've felt. A man, terrified, stuck with this kid. Shit. Shit. How do you blame a guy? A ticket out of there, and now what? Your life was over.

He felt old. Old and tired. Was this the sickness? Was this the first thing you felt when you got bit: *old?* All the damn stages of life, and now this one. The baby. His old man. Him—

The kid across the alley.

Jeffery sat up. Goddamit. Ten minutes left? Fuck.

He grabbed the baby and the stupid yuppie pack. The kid squealed as Jeffery pushed away from that busted sofa with its white foam guts hanging out. The ashes on the table stirred in his wake.

The door swung open, lock busted. He didn't pause to listen for the dragging of feet, didn't stop to sniff for that putrified smell that sometimes preceded an attack. He'd been through the building once before, and now it didn't matter. Fuck. How long? His foot hurt like a sonofabitch, worse than anything that'd earned him those two Purple Stars. He dripped blood and limped his way up crooked stairs that could somehow still command any damn rent they wanted. Third floor. He needed the third floor.

On the landing of the second, someone banged a door shut. Another survivor. They were like rats scurrying from the sounds of each other. People living on top of people and pretending they weren't there. Just like it'd always been. A hotel of strangers. The only sign of a neighbor the voices from their TVs seeping through ceiling and walls. Now, not even that.

Jeffery didn't call out, didn't ask for help. He didn't know this person, this rat. The kid across the alley. That's who. No one else.

He spotted the boy again from the old apartment. The bag of chips was still there, the window still open, ugly curtains fluttering like the building was still alive, still doing its thing. Across the way, the teenager was watching the scene in the alley, the boxed-in chompers agitated and confused, stuck like fish that'd swum into a net and couldn't figure how to get loose.

There was no clothesline from that apartment, just a jury-rigged wire for sharing cable TV, a pair of shoes hanging from its laces, a long-ago prank from laughing days.

Jeffery spotted a clothesline next door. He went down the hall to a place he'd cleared hours earlier. Putrified remains of a likely renter swung from an electrical wire in the bedroom, neck bulging. He'd taken the lazy way out. Jeffery ignored this, wondered vaguely if he'd be eating that mess in half an hour. Or maybe he'd be going after the survivor one floor down, that rat. He forgot about this and made sure the squirming kid was in the backpack, did the restraints up tight, swung him over his shoulders. Goddamn, his foot hurt. He could feel it working up past his knee. Five minutes? Goddamn.

The window wouldn't budge. Painted tight a long time ago. Jeffery didn't have time for this bullshit. He could see the clothesline right out by the fire escape, but he didn't want to go through the bedroom with the dangler, so he shoved his boot through the glass. He kicked the remaining shards out and beat the top pane with his fist to knock the hangers loose. He'd gotten good at this, he saw, busting in and out of places. Damn. A lot of talents wasted. Gone. Stupid.

He stooped real low to get outside, mindful of the kid on his back. The young man from across the way was watching him. Shit, this was a lot to saddle a young man with. A lot. Then again, giving life to someone weren't always a gift. You'd really done something when you knocked a girl up. Done something with lasting consequences. All the good and bad in a life, all set into motion with a mindless romp.

The kid watched him, chewing something. He had food. That was good. Must be a good kid to still be around. By now they were either the best of them or the worst of them. This kid didn't look like one of the worst of them.

The straps of the yuppie pack cinched tight to the line. There was a pair of red boxers flapping out there like some kind of flag, one of those messages the Navy cats used. Fuck, that was a different lifetime, all the fighting. This was something else.

The line squeaked around the white plastic pulley as Jeffery hauled the cord. The boxers jerked through the air like a fish, contracting as it dove forward, fins popping out when it paused. The baby with no name, a name lost with its momma, slid out after it. Squealing with delight, a cluster of foul motherfuckers down in the alley sniffing the air, the baby chased the red fish across the alley.

Jeffery looked up and saw that the kid from the window was gone. Damn, his shoulders were stiff. Fuck. Hard to move. He gritted his teeth and kept pulling in cord. Fingers would lock on the wire, but it was getting difficult to open them back up. Damn. Happening fast. Needed to sit down. Took work to breathe. Instead, he leaned against the creaky metal railing of the high fire escape and tried to grab more wire. A clothespin popped off out there in the alley and tumbled down into the orgy of undead. An infant bobbed, precarious, squealing faintly, hanging from a thread.

Jeffery couldn't move his arms. He sagged down on stiff and tired legs, collapsed back on his ass, his pulse in his foot, but not so much blood leaking out anymore.

Hungry. He thought about those potato chips, still crisp, but they didn't seem appetizing. He thought about that poor man swinging from a length of electrical wire in the other room, the one who'd given up, the dangler who took the lazy way. Meanwhile, an infant swung on a different wire, squealing, legs walking on empty air.

Goddamn.

The end comes slow so you can think about it. Jeffery thought of the soldier from another unit whose hand he'd held while he'd panted those thin gasps that you reckon for a man's last. He'd watched the life spiral out of that soldier while gunfire popped all around, helicopters saying it was too hot to land. Wasn't much later he'd been on the other end, fighting for his own lungful of air, squeezing the hand of an Iraqi militia man they were there to advise, there to hand off the deep shit to someone else, like generations coming one after another. An old man was hanging in the next room, a baby dangling from a wire, Jeffery sitting powerless in between. Nothing moving for a long moment. Nothing moving maybe ever again.

There was a squeak.

Jeffery figured it came from his own lungs, from the baby, from the dumpster far below. He'd seen that big brother with the missing finger start making noises after a period of quiet.

Another squeak.

Again.

It was the big wheel bolted to the brick, the wire sliding around. Jeffery couldn't move, but he could gaze through the rusted bars of that fire escape and watch the red fish dart through the air, contracting and spreading its fins. He watched the child swing after, tiny hands clutching the empty air, a good boy in a different window chewing something while he accepted the impossible. Chewing something. Pulling wire. While a hunger of a different sort took hold of the man formerly known as Jeffery Biggers.

Part IV ✦ The Leftovers

Rhoda Shay • Carmen Ruiz • Margie Sikes

30 ❖ Rhoda Shay

The streets of New York glittered like those rare moments after a sudden hailstorm. That slice of startled time when clouds part, the sun returns, and its light catches in a field of summer ice before hot pavement vanishes it into puddles. Rhoda had seen it happen a few times in the city, frozen balls the size of her thumb falling from the sky on a hot and humid day, a thing to puzzle over before it was gone and she was left wondering what had happened, something to call a friend to verify, to turn to Google for answers.

But this wasn't one of those long-ago days. It wasn't hail, this glittering field. It wasn't warm enough in the city for ice to fall from the sky. This was the weather of the apocalypse, the sign that the end times had arrived. It was streets of broken glass. Broken glass everywhere, and no one left to sweep it up.

Rhoda trudged through the glitter, unable to divert her course, and the shards crunched beneath her bare feet. The pain was intolerable, but that's precisely what she had to do: tolerate it. There was no choice, no motor function, not really. She couldn't even roll her feet to the outside to lessen the impact. The glass simply drove deep into her sensitive soles with every new shimmering puddle of it she crept through. Just a plodding shuffle, pure pain lancing up through her bones and into her knees, a constant flame held to the tenderness of her poor feet, all for not being adequately prepared.

She should've prepped differently. Rhoda kept berating herself for not prepping differently. All around her were people in shoes, some in boots, women in heels that had popped off their feet and clung to their ankles, the dainty straps like thin and desperate arms. They dragged along behind bare feet through pink-tinted glass.

There was a woman up ahead in trainers, glorious trainers. A man in work boots, a blue-collar and burly man that Rhoda would never have traded places with under any circumstances. But now. Oh, now. His steel-toed Hummers crunched through the glass oblivious to the pain, and this was all Rhoda could think about. Nerve endings burned throughout her body. The pain was up to her elbows. She thought of that guy from *Moonlighting* who'd gone bald and been in that movie, the one with the skyscraper. The scene of him sitting down and pulling clear daggers out of his feet, she couldn't stop picturing that scene. Rhoda had daggers like that right up against the bone, could feel her shredded flesh dragging across the pavement behind her in torn ribbons. Another glittering puddle ahead, and the scent was gonna drag her right through it. Shop glass: the worst. From a nearby storefront looted early on. There were real jewels in the window, absolutely worthless.

Worthless.

Rhoda's mind swung back and forth around what was valuable and what wasn't. She'd been through this once before, a breakdown just like this. And now somewhere, someone was probably coming across her stash. She feared they were finding what she'd hidden away, and at the same time: she hoped someone was. She hoped it wouldn't go to waste. She imagined them breaking into her apartment and finding her closet full of prepper gear, all the gear her friends had made fun of her for.

A closet full of supplies. Water, food, camping gear, purification tablets, protection, even a small generator that she ran once a week like the manual said. Exhaust hose shoved out the window, her tiny apartment smelling faintly of gas. There was a pump for pulling moisture out of the air that she could never quite get to work right, not the liter of potable fluid a day that it promised. There were the flashlights and a radio that she could wind up to power. Everything in her closet that her friends said she didn't need, not in New York City, that island of plenty.

They made fun of her for keeping her clothes in plastic crates, shoved under the bed, the bed she'd raised on cinder blocks to make more room. They'd made fun of her apartment, not quite 400 square feet, and a good bit of that devoted to the end times. They told her to live in the *moment*, the *now*. Rhoda had always smiled and kept her thoughts to herself. She knew. She watched the History channel, which was as good as any university, and she learned. She studied. She read all the books, the ones she had to order because the library didn't carry them.

And Rhoda got ready.

Her sister Charlotte had outed her at Thanksgiving two years back. Charlotte claimed to be worried about her, said she saw the stuff Rhoda was reading, or maybe she'd heard from her friends or spotted the pattern on Facebook. Whatever. She had grown concerned. And so she outed her right there in the kitchen in front of everyone. Rhoda's mom had been confused.

"I think it's fine that she dresses nice," her mother had said, peering into the oven to make sure she didn't burn the turkey like the year before.

"*Prepper*, mom," Charlotte had said, exasperated. "Not preppy."

Rhoda had argued and felt betrayed as Charlotte explained the differences. But their mother was impervious to either of their worries. While Charlotte stressed about where her sister was putting her money, Rhoda had much larger concerns. She tried to tell them all that could happen, explain to her mother and sister about the Mayans and how their calendar could be read so many different ways, that time could run out tomorrow or maybe ten years later. And didn't they know New York was due for the Next Big One? Or about the bees and their collapsing colonies? Or how water was running out, and the weather changing? Didn't they watch the news? Tornados were popping up everywhere. And look at what happened to the dinosaurs. Another impact like that, and every human being alive—

A stab of pain reminded Rhoda of the *now*, of the *moment*. It dragged her back from the past with an electrical shock shooting up her bare feet. She wore glass slippers. Glass crunching on glass. Soles embedded with a fine layer of what felt like razors drenched in alcohol. Needles into her heels, the flesh between her toes ripped and burning, glass caught between them and driving between the small bones there. Her feet were being mutilated. It felt like she was hobbling along on bare bone, on the ends of her shins.

The sight of others in shoes drove her mad. How one was shod when they got bit was important. Maybe this was the most important thing. It wasn't a detail that came up on the History channel, shaking her confidence in that learning institution. Unless she missed that show. Maybe she had. Boots, of course, she owned. Good ones. But she never wore them. They were stowed away in her closet, balls of white paper huddled inside, perfectly safe and snug, protected from the holocaust.

Her closet.

Rhoda imagined someone finding all her gear. The MREs and the jugs of water. Guns she'd only fired the once at a range. Stupid stuff. Before she'd started prepping, before she'd needed to put her bed on cinder blocks to make room, the closet had been full of clothes. It'd been full of shoes and belts and jewelry. Preppy stuff.

Her sister Charlotte had been no different, even back then. Always making fun of how she spent her money.

Laughing at her collection of shoes, some of them too painful to even wear, some of them that didn't go with a thing she owned or a night out she could possibly imagine having. And Charlotte had been right to make fun. Rhoda knew she had a problem. New York was a difficult place for a woman. So many windows full of tempting footwear, so dainty and perfect on their glass stands, beautiful just like that: Empty. Waiting. Footless.

There were shoes that felt perfect off the feet, their straps caught in the pads of her fingers while Rhoda strolled through the great lawn in Central Park. Shoes that looked perfect lying on their sides at the foot of the bed, ready to be donned and seen. Shoes that were wonderful simply in pairs of pairs of pairs at the bottom of her closet, lined up like soldiers. Perfect shoes, just knowing she *had* them.

But, instead of wearing them out to be seen, she stayed in and watched her little TV. And the shoes ate at her soul. Money wasted. Charlotte's voice. The end was coming, and she would be caught flat-footed. She wouldn't be ready. She was wasting her money. Her time. She needed to prepare.

When it finally and truly dawned on her, she'd made a drastic change. There had been a purge, and the purge had made Rhoda feel *alive*. Her friends were more than happy to come over and paw through her collection, seeing what fit, snagging designer heels at a fraction of the price. Rhoda watched them behave like animals. She watched from the bed, seeing herself as she had once been, digging through the aisles at Macy's on Memorial Day. She had been disgusted and relieved, seeing people she thought she knew behave like that. They paid her a fraction, and she took it gladly, the proceeds going to things that *mattered*. Rhoda would prepare for the worst. And when her few and sporadic dates came over after dinner or back from a bar, she would pray they wouldn't look inside her closet at the things she had chosen to accumulate.

More glass in the streets. Glass from smashed traffic and from storefront windows, glass from overhead where people had tossed furniture out of offices to make the only escape they knew how. Glass from bottles tossed for fun and dropped by looters, all picked up a shard at a time by tender flesh.

She should have known better, should have taken steps. But how would she have guessed that her mind would make this journey intact, that her flesh would rot, her nose wear away, while her every thought remained to haunt her?

Charlotte had been right: Rhoda had been a blasted idiot. She had wasted her money and time prepping to survive. Stomping heavily through that shimmering hell-storm, that weather of the apocalypse, she dwelled on all she'd done and the money she'd spent to prepare for her survival. When what she should've been readying for was what came *after*.

31 ❖ Carmen Ruiz

There were three of them still alive in the break room: Jackie, Sam, and Anna. Carmen could hear them talking through the door. She could smell them through the walls and through the vents. The two women cried while Sam tried to comfort them, but Carmen could smell the fear on him the worst. They talked and talked and filled the air with their ripe scents, no clue that the rest of the office could hear what they were saying, could smell what they were afraid of.

Carmen jostled among her coworkers outside the door, her belly swollen with an overdue baby and yesterday's grisly meal. She could flash back to eating Kassie or being bitten by Rhonda, but where does the blame start? Where does it stop? Each of them did what they were bound to do, and it probably went right back to the very first person with the sickness. Bit by a monkey in a lab somewhere, pricked by an experimental needle, a rip in a white suit, any of the scenes from all the films Carmen had seen.

However it started, there was a chain of blame that linked them all together. Carmen had been angry at the start, angry and scared, pissed at Rhonda, but those feelings had grown stale as the days piled up. Gruesome black bites marked the faces and arms of men and women she'd known for years, and it was getting hard to remember who had bitten whom. Those frantic days were long gone: the quarantine of the office, the handful who had tried to make it home, the cell phones clogged from overuse and then batteries dead from trying over and over anyway.

Now there were only three of them left, terrified and starving in the break room, and Carmen could hear them conspiring. They didn't know she and the others could understand. How could they? How could they know the monsters jostling outside the door were still aware of what was going on? Look at Mr. Helm, their asshole boss. He stumbled around in the dim hallway with the rest, eyes glazed over, shoulders hunched, a nasty wound on his chin where white bone peeked out between flaps of gray flesh. He looked as dead as the rest, but Carmen knew better. He was locked away just like her, trapped with his own demons, brushing up against the rest and hungry as hell.

The three of them inside the break room argued for the dozenth time about what to do. There had been five of them for a while. Louis had made a run for it. The idiot tried crawling through the ceiling, white flakes of Styrofoam or whatever the hell those panels were made of snowing down in drifts while he crept noisily overhead. Carmen had been one of the small pack to follow, sniffing after him. When the idiot broke through and crashed into Margarite's cubicle, she'd gotten a few bites in before the others crowded her away. And then there'd been four of them left to argue about what to do.

The three who now remained argued over the food, over how to get started. Anna said she wanted to start a fire. Sam called her a stupid bitch. He was from accounting, where Carmen imagined the phrase *stupid bitch* was common. He reeked of fear. Bullied the others. Carmen was hungry for him. She was hungry in general. Everyone was. But she had a baby inside her, taking up space, and maybe that made her more famished than the rest.

There were footsteps in the break room, the smell of Jackie approaching the door. She pounded on it with her fists. She yelled at those outside, almost as if she knew their souls were still trapped in there, as if she knew they would hear. But Carmen suspected she just needed to yell at something.

"Goddamn you!" Jackie screamed. "Let us go, you fuckers!"

Anna tried to calm her down. Sam told her to shut the fuck up. He said if they kept quiet, maybe the infected would leave. But Jackie knew what Carmen and the rest of the undead office knew: They weren't leaving. None of them were. Maybe not ever.

The survivors returned to their discussion in the break room. There were plastic forks and plastic knives. There had been five of them, now there were three. Louis had gotten himself eaten when he fell through the ceiling. Bits of him were all over Margarite's desk, smears on a monitor. On both sides of the break room door, there were groans from trapped and tortured souls. Sam told the girls that the plastic knives were a lot sharper than they looked. Anna wanted to build a fire. Sam told her she was a dumb bitch, that they would suffocate.

And so the shambling monsters of *Della, Baigaint & Padder* moved in agitated circles outside the break room. There was a smell in the air, a maddening smell. On the other side of the door, a starving trio continued to argue, even as they began to eat. There were five of them two days before. Carmen and the others had gotten one. Now she listened as Sam showed them just how sharp the plastic knives were, sharp enough to bite into flesh. Anna made gagging sounds. She wanted to build a fire. Jackie sobbed and filled the air with fear while Sam took the first bite.

There had been five of them, now three. Carmen shuffled in circles, her stomach full of unborn baby and the meat of her coworkers. And she wondered, listening to the survivors in the break room eat their gory meal, how the barred door between them made them any different.

32 ❖ Margie Sikes

There was a boy in the back seat, no more than fifteen or sixteen, and not for the first time, Margie Sikes found herself feeding on the young. She ripped the poor boy apart, him kicking and screaming and pleading for her to stop, tears rolling down his unblemished cheeks, Margie trying her best not to think of what she was doing.

The boy had been cornered car-hopping. Margie had seen it before, had even seen it work a time or two. Survivors ran through the streets and dove into intact cars while they waited for the wind to shift and lure the infected away. She'd seen it work up close. A good seal on a car, and the smell of its contents would eventually fade. It was maddening to be driven off by a fickle breeze. In her mind, she knew a good meal lay cowering on the floorboard of that SUV, but her brain would catch a whiff elsewhere, and try as she might to urge herself to stay and wait the hopper out, her feet would carry her inanely upwind toward some other struggling soul.

The smart hoppers stuck with the newer model vehicles. Tempered glass. Better seals and gaskets around the doors. And if there was space in the parked traffic and keys in the ignition, one might even roar to life and go on a spree or just sit and run the heat for a while. The sprees were something to watch. Besides the distant helicopters and the wildlife, the streets were a dull and lifeless place. The only movement was that of a rotting corpse shuffling behind storefront glass or in a restaurant full of tipped chairs and tangled bones. To see an exhaust sputter in the crisp fall air, hear an engine roar, watch a grille smack down a few of her own—it was exhilarating to Margie. She was just happy to be whatever she was. Not-quite-dead. Senses intact. Here, for however much longer.

The boy in the old gray sedan stopped screaming, but his limbs continued to move as Margie tore into his abdomen. Arms that waved feebly with the last of his young life. Groans and murmurs escaping his lips, but he made them insensibly. These were the noises people made in deep comas, tiptoeing along that narrowing ledge that everyone scooted across, a ledge that eventually melded into flat stone high above a deep and shadowy ravine.

Glass from the sedan's shattered window gouged into Margie's stomach as she bent over the door and worked on the boy. She had a grandson this kid's age. Nathan, her eldest daughter's boy. Margie wondered if upstate New York was similarly cursed. She tended to think it wasn't. That part of New York was a world apart. They shouldn't even share a name, the city and the state. Two completely different things. Like the difference between the living and whatever Margie had become.

Others in her pack jostled behind her, fairly roaring in frustration. They clawed at her and the air, which was heady with the scent of a feed. It was a private snack for Margie, who was swifter than most. Always at the front. Always first to dine. She stuffed herself with the soft and easy meat in the boy's stomach. She deserved it. It was she who had gotten him open.

The human body was a tricky thing to tear into without the proper tools. It reminded Margie of her honeymoon in Puerto Rico nearly sixty years ago, trying to get into that coconut. It wasn't until a local showed her husband how to strike it on a rock, peel back the husk, then crack the nut on some sharp edge that they'd gotten the knack of it.

With a body, she'd found, the first bite was the hardest. Trickier than you'd think. A flat abdomen could have teeth scraped across it to no effect. Fat around the middle made it easier, but the easy kills were gone or had wasted down to bone. A bite along the ribs usually gave purchase. Once a hole was started, like digging that first finger into the skin of an orange, the rest could be gradually peeled away. It was a pain, however, when the orange was kicking you in the chest and clawing at your eyes. But the hunger always found a way.

Margie stuffed herself with the choice bits before she was crowded out. Glass from the old window broke off in her abdomen. The pack roared forward. A fat old woman grabbed some of the intestine hanging from Margie's fist and chewed on that. A man caked in yesterday's blood dove for Margie's face to lick around and inside her mouth, lapping at the blood Margie was still trying to swallow. She recoiled in horror at this, and luckily her body did as well, lurching away from the man, a maggot stuck in her gums that must've come from him. The pack swelled in size and crowded close, and Margie was lucky to be squeezed toward the perimeter. There was the loud crack of more glass shattering. Someone began wasting their time going for the brains through the other door, that frustrating and alluring coconut.

As she stumbled away, overly full, Margie shat herself. There was no telling which feed it was, if it was the girl from yesterday or the old man from two days ago that ran down her legs. No one to sponge her. Staggering down the street, giddy and drunk from a feed, Margie thought of her old nurse and how what had seemed miserable in the days of the before was now a luxurious dream. Someone to bathe her, a feeding delivered on a plastic tray—old humiliations she would now kill for.

She passed a Bank of America with an odd scene, a man infected and stuck inside the glass ATM room, all alone. There were smears across the glass where he'd bumped against it or banged with his fists, a spread of gore from a long-ago feed. He gazed hungrily past Margie at the crowd in the streets. He was trapped there by the sudden loss of electricity, probably aware of what it would take to pry his fingers in the sliding doors and pull them aside, but unable to communicate this to his limbs. Margie felt bad for him.

He was stuck in there forever. She thought again of that coconut.

Another faint scent pulled her past the ATM. It was difficult to nose over the fresh blood dripping from her chin. Ironically, the smell seemed to point toward the hospital, her old hospital. She thought of her nurse and the nice doctors there, helping her through those last years, a service that had become expected. Seven hundred dollars a day. More, when there were procedures. Gobs more when the procedures had complications.

Margie thought of her eldest daughter upstate and her grandson Nathan. Insurance covered much of it. Her savings and Carlos's pension helped with the rest. It was a nest egg, a pile of nuts squirreled away that once tapped into was easy to keep chewing away at. Margie remembered watching those savings dwindle as she lay in bed, a daily sponge bath, re-runs on the TV in the corner, keeping her alive for another day. Another day just like the one before. Every day precious and miserable.

Margie pictured Nathan as she had last seen him, standing there beside her bed, fidgeting and glancing from the TV to the door. The boy had wanted to be anywhere else but standing there, that close to death. His nose had that wrinkle of someone scared to contract a disease. Margie wondered how much more disgusted he would have been had he'd known his college education was keeping her alive. Keeping her around to watch one more re-run, get one more bath.

She thought of the boy in the gray sedan near to Nathan's age. Kicking. Screaming. Begging her to stop. As if she had any choice, any say in the matter. It was the way things worked. And so Margie Sikes lumbered down 68th, a faint smell in the air, a boy in her belly, remembering the times she had senselessly fed on the young.

33 ✤ Carmen Ruiz

Forty-eight hours. A mere two days. That was the difference. Two days before they would've induced labor, before they would've stopped waiting. There was a time set—she'd written it down—her baby would be born, or begin to be born, at two o'clock, right on the dot.

Dot. Dotty. Dorothy.

Carmen still hadn't decided on a name. They kept coming to her, every one imperfect. And now, it wouldn't matter. Maddie. Madeline. She liked that one.

Something in Carmen's belly moved. At least, she thought it did. It was impossible to tell. Her limbs were lifeless and yet full of some other life. Both dead and animated, her arms and legs stirred beyond her control. She wanted dearly to rub her belly, to feel her baby kick. Other times, she wanted it to be still.

Two days.

If she hadn't been bitten by Rhonda, there would already be a new person in the world. A little baby to demand a name. If Carmen hadn't been bitten, she probably would've given birth in the office building somewhere, maybe locked up in the break room with Anna and the others.

A scene played out in her head: Sam delivering the baby, Anna mopping her head with water from the cooler, Jackie holding her hand—

No, that wouldn't work. The water from the cooler was almost out. They wouldn't waste what was left on her.

She imagined lying on the floor, knees spread before her coworkers, the tile running red around her with amniotic fluid and blood and who knew what else. It was easy to imagine such a scene. Blood ran down her legs already from what she'd done to Alice. Two cubicles over for the last five years, and now she was the stickiness beneath Carmen's maternity dress. Now Carmen's belly bulged with more than one life.

The carpet beneath her feet was threadbare and stained. Coffee, ink toner, blood, cigarette burns, all from the past weeks: the panic, the fighting, the feeding. She roamed the same patches, the same winding circuit as the others, shuffling across a carpet that told stories, some gory impressionist painting.

Manet. What a beautiful name.

All around her, throughout the sea of neatly cubed personal spaces with their shoulder-high walls, the scent of the barely living stirred through lifeless vents and ducts. The odor caused Carmen and the others to gyre like leaves and sticks in a stream's eddy, trapped but always moving.

Always moving.

A mere two days.

If she hadn't insisted on working right up to the last moment, she might've been in Jersey with her mom right then. No bite. A doctor delivering her baby instead of Sam in the break room, instead of whatever would happen now. A hospital with food, water, the unimaginable glory of juice or any meal but meat. She'd be able to brush her teeth whenever she wanted. Take a shower. Talk. Say her baby's name, hear what it sounded like in her ears rather than her mind. She couldn't even whisper a name.

But she had insisted on working—she'd bragged about working right up to the last moment. She had fantasized about her water breaking at her desk. *See? This was serious.* An ambulance would come. A procedure had been scheduled. Maybe they would have to cut her open. It would require surgery.

So much to prove. So much guilt about being a mom, the maternity leave, the imagined whispers and the words she placed behind every glance at her belly. All Carmen could think of was the incredible amount of work the baby would mean for her, but what she imagined was everyone else thinking: *Vacation. Leave time. Unfair. More work for us.*

So much guilt. For what? For bringing life into the world?

Carmen fumed as her powerless meandering took her into Mr. Helm's office. There was a vent in there that still oozed the smallest hint of life, probably from the break room, maybe from Louis's antics in the ceiling. Bumping around the wide desk, arms wavering in front of her, she made a circuit past the tall windows, an executive's reward for years of service, for never moving on to something better.

Through the expanse of glass, she spotted Jersey. Across the Hudson, where no boats stirred, no barges or ferries, the sun twinkling on ripples that gave her a sense of the forgotten and inaccessible wind. The buildings across the water stood like silent observers, like tourists huddled against a railing, their windows peeping eyeballs that scanned unblinking this new disaster across the way.

Carmen looked hard for signs of life while she had the chance. She scanned the shore, looking for little blips of people with binoculars, men talking into radios with a plan for saving them all, but it was perfectly still.

Perfectly still.

Hudson was a good name for a boy. Knowing the sex would be nice. It would narrow it down. But Carmen wanted to be surprised. She told everyone the child was a surprise.

Lumbering around the desk, she lost the view and stared at a wall, a calendar of appointments, a clock that still ticked on its little batteries. What did that glimpse of the far shore tell her? No movement. And what still moved anymore? Only the dead.

So Jersey must be alive, Carmen decided. Or was that simply what she wanted to believe? It was counterintuitive, this idea that stillness meant life and that movement across the water would just signify more shuffling and unthinking souls. This could be her wishful thinking, but she truly believed Jersey was alive for being able to remain quiet, able to hold its breath, to fall still. Jersey, and perhaps the rest of the country. Carmen thought it was just Manhattan that had succumbed. This is what she had pieced together with that occasional view. The rest were pulling back, keeping their distance, still able to choose where to go and choosing to go away.

Two days.

That's how long, and she would've been there pulling back with them, clutching her precious baby, reading the headlines, wondering what horrible things her friends were going through, feeling guilty perhaps for leaving work, for leaving them behind to have a baby she always said she never wanted.

But no. She was here. And her legs were sticky with the guts of a friend. Her dress was a bib of gore. The flesh on her one hand was rotting away, charred black where Rhonda had gotten her through the door and the others had left her to become something else. And in her belly, in her belly, something stirred. A nameless baby moved.

It moved, she was sure of that now. And what still moved? What moved anymore in that wretched place?

It was counterintuitive, she knew. Or maybe it was just her fears. Carmen asked herself this question over and over as she lumbered around the island of cubicles once more, bumping into her coworkers, all of them dead just like her. Dead, and still moving. The only things that moved anymore.

34 ❖ Rhoda Shay

clack. clack. thwump.

Central Park was covered in frost. Overgrown and unruly grass let off steam as the ground warmed, the sun slanting through trees oblivious to the ruin of the city all around this green patch. The trees stood as motionless sentinels in the calm air of daybreak, dark shapes flitting between their boughs, birds calling to one another, still thinking about sex and territory and food while monsters roamed below.

clack. thump.

Fallen and crisp leaves rustled with squirrels. Inured as ever to the presence of people, they sat on their haunches, cheeks twitching, and watched Rhoda stumble by. Desperately hungry, she occasionally lurched toward them when they ranged too close, but the squirrels could bolt out of reach in an instant. Her body felt as mindless and ineffectual as a dog, always thinking the next try would nab the impossible. Around a thick tree, two squirrels chased one another in furry spirals of clicking and scratching claws, a much more even match. Too even. They would never catch each other or truly get away.

clack. clack.

The joggers were the only thing missing. The joggers and those early risers who found the time to sit on park benches with coffees and newspapers and bagels, their suits and dresses lending them the air of the gainfully employed. Rhoda guessed it was between six and eight. The sun normally rose while she was slapping the snooze button or waking up in the shower. Of all the many and new powerless things, not knowing the time was just another. No cell phone to glance at. No one to ask. In ancient times, she imagined people just knew how far along the day was. One glance at the spinning constellations, and it was time to plant or harvest or head south.

Rhoda's constellations had vanished. She didn't even know they were there until they were gone. There were the joggers in the morning that let her know she would be early to work, kids being walked to school by their parents or older siblings, trucks squeaking to a stop by curbs so burly men could unload boxes of food and cases of beer. There were the subways full of people hurrying for trains, the express packed so full that the last ones in had to laugh, their skirts flapping between the rubber seals as the conductor—after four or five tries to get the doors together—finally zipped them away from the station.

thump.

There were the nighttime stars that gave her the hour as well. The crush that spread from Times Square when the shows let out. The boys and girls in tight jeans flowing to and from Brooklyn in the wee hours, looking for somewhere hip to hang out. The city changed by the hour. It changed by the day. The flower district seemed to explode more lushly on Tuesdays and Thursdays. The streets fell quiet on the weekends, the cabs thinning to a yellow trickle for much of the morning. Time. Taken for granted. Everything changing until it didn't, until the sameness stirred memories of the way things used to be.

clackclack. clack. thwump.

Rhoda enjoyed the walk through the park. The glass in her feet didn't press so hard, and there was less of it to pick up. She watched a young girl chase a squirrel through the woods. The girl moved fast for one of the dead, was either recently turned or mad with hunger. Rhoda wanted to call out that it was no use, to leave the poor things alone, but she probably wouldn't even if she could. It wasn't as if the girl had a choice.

The sun rose while she walked aimlessly. That distant star no longer lit the undersides of the tall trees, but began to dribble light down through them. Rhoda passed the wide streets where cars were not allowed, the separate paths for bikes and anything on wheels. The joggers were the only thing missing from the hour. There was just one man, a pathetic man on rollerblades, sitting on his ass with a haunting and bewildered look on his ashen face. One of his arms was broken and flopped with an extra elbow as he tried to push himself up. There would be something comical about his plight if Rhoda didn't know that a man was still inside there. Still trapped. Locked in the hour. He was like a broken clock that only felt right once a day as the rising sun came to him.

She watched him struggle and felt like weeping, imagining what it must be like to be locked in that head, strapped to those skates, pushing down with an arm that gave way where arms shouldn't.

A young girl chased a squirrel and ran face-first into a tree, and nothing about that was funny to Rhoda.

The man in skates tried once more to get up, but the hour for skating had passed him by. What remained was sad and pathetic, an awful drumbeat beneath the singing birds, a sound that faded as Rhoda chased a scent of the living world she once knew and was starting to forget.

clack. clack.

thump.

35 ❖ Margie Sikes

Margie chased the living down the street, her old bones moving better than they had in decades. The survivors had squeezed through a gap between two buildings, another group of undead flushing them out. She moved as quickly as she could, her legs rotting and yet not falling apart as they once had. This was something different. Now, she could practically totter. It felt so fast. Dozens of others shuffled along behind, a few keeping up. The running meat, five survivors, were hurrying through an alley a block and a half away.

Margie could picture them, even though they weren't yet in sight. She'd seen enough survivors clutching their belongings and glancing over their shoulders with wide eyes. They were invariably thin and gaunt, looking like how Margie felt. Hunger drove them out. It stirred the living much as it moved the dead. For weeks, these survivors had taken to scurrying like roaches through the impressive towers of glass and steel, scrounging for crumbs, avoiding the slow horrors in the hallways and cubicles until the primal need for food or water forced them out into the streets.

Margie remembered. She remembered her own time hiding out, scrounging, getting up from a bed she had long fibbed about not being able to leave.

This group of five made a now familiar dash. They ran from one island tower to the next, the streets between like shark infested waters. Margie could smell each one of them like a distinct meal. Her hunger noted their hunger, this trotting meat marinating in a hormonal blend of fear and panic that she longed to taste.

Another pack emerged from an alley; they stopped and turned what was left of their soft noses into the breeze, half circles of bone visible beneath their haunted eyes. Holes where noses once lay groped for the scent, for the smells that had become something like flavored ropes in the air. These holes in rotting heads grasped for scented threads that led back to their source, to the meat running and clutching their belongings.

The world looked different and strange to Margie. She could see the odors in the air. This was how prey saw the world, she thought. This was how deer made scarce when man intruded. They *knew* long before they could see.

A small pack of undead lumbered after the survivors. Larger and slower armies converged from all over. There was no escape. Just a matter of time. Who ate and who didn't. Who went hungry and who got a nick and managed to get away to become something worse than starvation.

The others, the slow, they were converging. The meal would be hemmed in.

Margie went as fast as her body could, passing a few less fortunate, the longer-since dead, those with clumsy wounds. Her body was degrading as well. Only a matter of time. She caught sight of her arms and hands as she hurried along, the holes in the flesh only half the story. The soft parts of her were going to waste on the inside as well. Bone rubbed on bone where tendons and cartilage used to lie. At times, Margie squeaked. Her curse had taken hold a week ago, give or take. The senseless nights made it difficult to be sure. Others in her pack fared better or worse, rotted more swiftly or slowly. It was a puzzle, everything a puzzle. Something to keep her mind occupied.

The group of five was going to emerge from the alley ahead. Margie could smell them coming. They had chosen to make their break in the predawn hours. Smart. The wind was at its most calm during the break of day. Scents were relatively feeble. But then, the living had no idea the traces they left, the odors they put out, how the molecules swam through the air. For them, it was all guessing. She remembered guessing like this, back before she knew.

Two females and three males. Even out of sight, she could nose them. She followed. Not followed, moved to intercept. They were coming toward her, half a block away. There was a surge of panic and disappointment in the air as one of their number tried a door and couldn't get in. The living made it hard on their fellow man—their barricades were everywhere. It was only the desperate starvation that drove them to this. The last of the candy from smashed vending machines, another water cooler bled dry, that secret stash in a nurse's bottom drawer of Cheetos and diet cola, the cramps and headaches from meals of sugar and little else.

Margie remembered. The hospital had descended into chaos. Food lying around everywhere, but not for the living. Food lying in beds, watching TVs.

Her small pack broke out of the alley and across 6th, the *Avenue of the Americas*. Street signs seemed pointless with all the unmoving cars. No one was going anywhere. She moved to intercept five students of this lesson, five who were about to learn. The end of them was inevitable. She had seen it play out too often the past weeks and from both sides. Sometimes she rooted for the living when they made a break for it—but pity turned to contentment as the meat was corralled. The living made mistakes, simple ones from her vantage, the same mistakes she'd made and that the man in the ragged overcoat beside her must've made, that *all* of them in her pack had made. Dire mistakes that now made sense. Hidden secrets, which seemed suddenly clear. Give her a second chance with what she now knew, give back her youth and this knowledge, and Margie thought she'd make it. She'd be one of those she heard about in rumors who swam the Hudson or East River to safety. She'd be one of those.

The small group of survivors spotted her pack as they emerged from the alley. Margie scurried after them. The living twitched in a way that made them stand out from their surroundings. Everything else swayed and lurched, lurched and swayed, the dragging of limbs, the pendulum swing of darkened stoplights, the dance of debris caught up in the wind. But meat alive had a raw panic in its joints. Heads turned this way and that, noses blind, eyes scanning the littered streets, wary of danger.

Two of the men in the group wrestled with a door while a pair of women supported a third man, who seemed to be the one filling the air with blood smells. There were plenty of buildings wide open, plenty of gaping maws bashed in with glittering and ragged teeth. But these were both ransacked and infested. Margie remembered. A group of five didn't last this long without learning a few things. She found herself rooting for them a little more as her pack closed in.

They were smart, this group, but time was running out. Others were out sniffing for a meal. Margie spotted the rhythmic lumbering of their approach from a block north, a pack twice the size of her own. They would converge, she saw. The two men rattled the door, desperate to get inside. They knew better than to bash it down with a trashcan, to destroy the walls they would soon need. The smell of the bleeding one was intoxicating. Margie was near the front of her pack, joints squeaking, angling through the frozen traffic, piles of clean bones scattered across front seats, just half a block away.

Margie could see the wide eyes on the girls, the whispering and urgent lips. Too skinny, these survivors.

She wondered if these women had been too skinny to begin with. The men wrestled with the door and watched both packs grow nearer, the dead closing like a vise. They were being stupid, now. It was time to run. Time to grab one of those steel trashcans and bash a hole through perfect teeth. The time for smart was petering out.

A hundred feet away. The bleeding man hopped on one foot, scanning the doom lumbering at his group from all sides. A third pack tumbled around the corner from 22nd. This would be a big feed, an ugly one. Five bodies and five hundred mouths. Margie felt a rush of dread even as she quickened her squealing and squeaking pace. Two of her fingers had disappeared in a feed like this, back in those first days. She still wasn't sure if she'd done it herself or if it'd been a neighbor. Her brain had wandered into some kind of orgasmic state, the feed witnessed through a straw of awareness, pure pleasure squeezing down around her. She moved now as fast as she could, wishing she could turn and run the other way, confused by the stupidity of the men wrestling with that unyielding door.

Paces away, now. Packs converging. The roar of pure hunger, of intense starvation, like waves crashing on a beach. Margie marveled for the millionth time at this city that could not feed itself, these towering islands reliant on daily deliveries, reefers idling along the curb, men with carts pushing boxes of food from open farmland over the rivers and a distant world away. No more than two or three days of food stockpiled on the island, isn't that what someone had told her? And it had been run through quickly. And now these poor and ragged things were being swarmed by sharks as they hunted for a scrap or two.

Margie nosed ahead of the others. A man wearing the remnants of a business suit at the head of the opposite pack would beat her to them, but there was enough meat for them all. Here was where rooting for the survivors ended, where her own needs took over. The world around her narrowed as she anticipated the orgasmic feast. The five survivors were surrounded, walking corpses staggering between all the parked and wrecked cars, every avenue of escape writhing with the undead, closing on the wide-eyed and the stupid, stupid meat.

Movement inside the glass building was mistaken for a reflection at first. But it was the hurry and twitch of the living. One of the men by the door shouted to the heavens, a curse or a blessing or a command.

Margie was near enough to taste them when the wires went taut. The bleeding man straightened, the women stepped away, angry fire replacing the fear in their eyes. Margie groped ahead of herself, pawing the air, as the group floated up, sneakers squeaking on a wall of glass, the shouts from concerted others a few stories up, their smells drifting down as the overpowering scent of the bleeding man faded.

Three packs converged. Margie was hungry enough to eat the man in the tattered business suit, whose flesh had not been rotting for long, might still taste alive. They bumped and jostled while wires sang and sneakers squeaked. There was movement inside the building.

Margie watched. She saw her own reflection, the hideous condition of herself, half naked and dilapidating, a hole in her skull where her nose had been, what flesh remained already old and wrinkled and revolting from a life much too long in the living. And beyond her reflection, a man with fire. A twinkling fuse, a rag like a candle. Legs that could still run, fading deep into her reflection, disappearing into the building's hallway guts.

The merging packs formed a crush of rot, the heady scent of blood and flesh replaced by the stench of the unburied dead, the blood and shit and half-digested flesh in their pants and under their skirts, the groans vibrating through the mass as they all pushed in toward an empty and confusing feed.

Margie was pinned against the glass, the living scampering above to safety, a drop or two of sacrificial blood plummeting down from the heavens.

The fuse shortened. The candle burned down to the red jug stenciled with the word "gas." Margie tried to scream, her loose flesh coming off as she was smeared against the window, remembering how stupid she'd been. Remembering.

Until, in a flash, she could remember no more.

36 ❖ Carmen Ruiz

There was a stabbing pain in Carmen's gut like the twist of a knife. She felt her knees wobble and very nearly buckle as the thing in control of her responded to a hurt for once. Her body seemed startled by the sensation. A few steps more, and the jolt came again. Her chin dipped toward the source, eyes falling to her swollen belly protruding naked and taut between her sagging skirt and bunched-up blouse. It was dim on the back side of the cubicles near the copier room, but she could see her protruding bellybutton like a small thumb sticking from her belly.

Another lance, a lightning bolt, and Carmen's shoulder bumped into the wall and knocked a motivational poster loose, the cheap frame bouncing to the floor. Donald from the sales department lumbered past, sniffing at the air, jostling against her. His face was a mess of parallel gashes from where a colleague had put up a fight. His head turned to follow Carmen as she staggered past. Her pain was intolerable.

Carmen regretted the lies. She thought Donald and the others could smell it on her, the lie of this pregnancy. She worried that her mother knew, that everyone knew this thing inside her was no accident, but rather a planned and pathetic secret.

The pain in her belly sent Carmen back to a game she used to play, a soothing game. Alone in the sandbox or at the beach, she remembered the calming scoops of sand, the way its cool heft conformed to her hand. Carmen used to love spilling that sand from palm to palm, marveling at the dwindling supply no matter how carefully she tried to catch it all. A mound would become a trickle, a pinch, and then a mere row of tiny grains caught in the two lines of her young hands.

She banged into the water cooler stand, the empty bottle long since knocked free, as pure agony dragged her from past to present like a dog shaking a toy with its teeth.

The game. The loose fist. Sand running out through the curl of her pinky to fall and pile up in her other palm. So careful and exacting, but it all disappeared. Forty passes, maybe fifty, the wind snatching it away invisibly.

A lurch in Carmen's belly. A kick. The game had gone from soothing to sad as she grew older. She began to see it everywhere, could feel life mimic this obsession of hers. Time slipped away in a familiar manner, and love dwindled as it was tossed back and forth in the form of arguments. It could only go away, everything she saw and everywhere she looked. Money. It disappeared from her accounts no matter how hard she tried to save. Time and love and wealth and anything worth building or wrapping one's arms around, trying to hold on to it all, eroding like the cascade of sand between two palms, stolen by the breeze.

Carmen was punched in the gut. She saw the thumb-like button of flesh protruding from her belly. A malformed hand was going to come out right where that button was, a tiny claw ripping her open from the inside. Carmen could feel her baby gnawing on her organs. At least, that's what she thought this was. The pain was her little monster chewing through her, a grotesqueness that would emerge from her skin like some horror movie.

She silently wept.

She imagined her precious baby eating its way through her flesh and falling to the ground, helpless. She pictured it dragging behind her on its slimy cord, wailing and ignored, until it caught on the edge of a cubicle as she turned a corner.

Oh fuck, oh fuck, oh fuck.

She was scared enough being alone, having this baby by herself, her and some anonymous donor. She was terrified and tired from keeping the lies straight, the stories of one-night stands and ex-boyfriends, of not wanting anything to do with the father. The truth was pathetic: she just needed someone in her life, a person who couldn't choose to go away.

Oh fuck. That someone was coming. A rage formed in her powerless limbs, a shuddering violence beneath her skin. It was that feeling she got in her legs sometimes, the need to shake them, to move them, but no amount of activity made the sensation go away. So she would try and hold still, to ride it out, but the pain would grow and grow until she was forced into paroxysms of jitteriness that still didn't touch the need, that still left her feeling cramped with something worse than broken bones.

Carmen wanted to shout. She wanted to plunge from some great height. The torture in her abdomen grew worse. Her baby was alive. Both alive and undead. And she would not be giving birth to it so much as watching it emerge unbidden from a tear in her flesh.

A wave of blackness, pain so intolerable that Carmen came to on the carpet. Her body struggled to right itself. She moved to her knees, began to stand. And then a sudden release, another surprise urination, warm and sticky running down her legs.

Donald circled back and stood over her. Harris was there, kicking through spilled paperwork. The smell of blood, not urine, was in the air.

Her knees gave out once more, her shoulder striking the ground. She flopped onto her back. In the dim space between the cubicles and the copier room, Carmen lay gazing up at the ceiling, at the hole Louis had fallen through. There was the smell of blood in the air, the ripe smell of a thing alive in a space long devoid of such a scent. Pressure between her legs, the throb of something like a pulse, but Carmen had no pulse. She couldn't see. Oh fuck, what was happening to her? She couldn't see, but could feel a thing, a solid thing, press between her thighs. And she thought she heard, maybe, just barely, the cry of her unnamed child as its lungs filled with air for the first time, born into utter hell, not undead at all.

She thought she heard the cry. It was impossible to tell. All was drowned out by the hungry gurgles and shuffling feet as her coworkers converged on their prize, on this thing they had secretly hated her for and now desired to have for their own.

37 ❖ Rhoda Shay

The eating wasn't too bad. It was better than the walking. It meant kneeling down and taking the weight off her glass slippers. And besides, as foul as the taste was, Rhoda had prepared for this. Life in the aftermath meant eating for sustenance, not for pleasure. It meant holding one's breath and forcing down dry and pre-packaged meals. It meant eating bugs, which Rhoda had done in abundance to prepare herself. Six times, she had taken that tour with the smelly guy from Craigslist who for twenty bucks would turn over logs in Central Park and show you what you couldn't and couldn't eat. They tasted like peanuts, he said, and Rhoda hadn't believed him. Just like peanuts. He'd been right. The power of suggestion, perhaps.

Rhoda told herself that this feast would be like sushi. It was a game show. All she had to do to win a million dollars was gobble it down and keep it down. Which she knew wouldn't be a problem, she just needed to forgive the taste.

Two jumpers. She'd seen the remnants of another jumper a week ago, but it'd been at night and after a soft rain and much of the mess was gone before her nose led her to the smear. This was fresh. Two others were already there, lapping up pink globs amid scraps of clothes. The bodies had exploded, the clothing shredded. Like a bomb going off. Maybe they'd gone from the top. A man and a woman, judging by the clotted tangle of hair at the end of one mess and the beard on what looked like a chin a pace away.

The insides were everywhere. Made it easy. Like finding a buffet on the pavement. Scrambled human. Rhoda fell to her knees, so thankful to her body for doing so, and the pressure and pain in her mangled feet lessened. The perpetual burning became a distant hum. Eating meant forgetting these other things. Being disgusted lessened her physical pain.

A crowd headed their way in the distance. Rhoda ate while she could. Two jumpers. She wondered if they'd gone together, a lover's leap. Maybe they'd held hands. It was hard to tell where their hands were. The man's arm had split open like a lobster tail cooked too long, a neat rupture from impact, a baked potato with all the fixings.

This was ketchup, Rhoda said to herself as she buried her nose in the gash and ate. She chewed down to the bone—the *plate*, she corrected herself. It wasn't bad. The constant jolt of electricity in her feet receded to a thrum. It was amazing what one ill could do for another. Amazing what could be justified.

Rhoda ate her way from the man to the woman, ate in that place where the two mingled. The birds plucked scraps of flesh from a dozen feet away, little pink worms. They squawked at each other as the crowds grew closer, and Rhoda thought of the jumpers she'd seen on TV once. Little black shapes falling. Like swooping birds. They caught her eye before the anchor noticed, before the cameraman zoomed in. Yes, those where what the anchorman thought they were. A jacket rippling in the wind, trailing the falling man like a shadow, peeled away as it left one arm and then the other.

Several of them. She had watched, horrified, while they showed it live. A man in a pike position, head at his knees, turning over and over.

Rhoda never understood why.

Why?

Why jump?

But now she knew. It was the glass in her feet, the little shards of wisdom grinding into her bones. She ate warm muscle, teeth scraping on the insides of the skin—a baked potato, she reminded herself. It wasn't that bad. Not as bad as the walking.

Rhoda remembered the jumpers. Why leap like that? Because the sitting had to've been worse. Trapped in there, the heat intolerable, mangled bodies of people they'd worked with for years, getting hotter and hotter. The only relief was by the shattered windows, the breeze that sucked at the wrecked filing cabinets, the whoosh of winds high above the streets.

Cool by the window, but growing warmer. Fires advancing. No way out. Like slippers of glass and just wanting to fall to one's knees, to do anything but suffer.

Rhoda ate. If she could have done it with grace, she would have. She pictured herself in a glorious pike, high over a shimmering pool of water, flying down like the swooping bird that stopped, cawed, and with its perfect beak, caught the eye of that plummeting jumper.

Part V ✤ The Lippmans

38 ✦ Darnell Lippman

Darnell told Lewis something like this would happen. She told him. Probably happened all the time. Who knew how often New York City went through this sort of thing without word ever reaching Homer? Alaska was practically a world apart. The East Coast was a foreign land where their days slipped by before Darnell's had even begun. Coming here was his idea. He wanted to see Ground Zero, see the new tower going up, had found a deal on tickets. But Darnell had *told* him something like this would happen. She knew it. They'd get crushed by the traffic, mugged, lost, separated. She knew they'd get separated, torn apart by the crowds. She wouldn't be able to find him and would be stranded there forever, she knew it. And now look.

As soon as they'd landed, she'd had this feeling. Was it three weeks ago? It was in Times Square, that's when the real panic had started, when she just *knew* she'd lose him.

They'd taken a cab straight from the airport, suitcases and all. Lewis said he couldn't wait, said they could just walk to the hotel from there. He'd wanted to see this since he was a kid, all the lights and those big video screens. It was where the New Year was ushered in. Prematurely, as far as Darnell was concerned. A new year just in time for dinner back in Homer.

But Darnell had gone along just like she always did. Anything to see him happy. But the crowds! The throngs. Streets packed from sidewalk to sidewalk, closed to traffic, and not even a holiday! Just the regular mob. The daily flow. As crazy as if salmon spawned year-round, like flapping fish that didn't know when to quit.

She had chased him for blocks, her suitcase swerving behind her and nearly twisting out of her grip, wrist still sore from getting through that crazy airport with a bazillion foreigners, losing sight of him over and over, his balding head a tiny raft bobbing on a sea of pedestrians.

And that's why the green hat she'd bought him. The "I LOVE NY" hat that used a heart in place of "LOVE." Darnell made him stop right there in Times Square and try it on. She told him it was his color. She told him he needed it, that he looked so handsome.

Lewis asked if he was going bald, if that had anything to do with the sudden interest. She told him "no." The street vendor took their money and stopped Lewis from taking the sticker off the brim, said he was supposed to leave that on. Lewis narrowed his eyes, and Darnell knew he would be peeling it off as soon as he got away. She didn't care.

All she wanted was a bright canopy on that bobbing raft, a flag on his head like the one that always helped her spot his boat when he pulled back into the harbor.

They had dragged their suitcases—still cool from the altitude—through a New York night throbbing with neon and noise and a frightening amount of life. And Darnell had watched for the green hat. She had followed along, a few paces behind, no idea where they were going, no idea what she would do if they got separated. Would he hear his phone ring over all that noise? Would she know how to hail a cab? She didn't even know where the hotel was. This was her nightmare, the flashing billboards, videos and commercials the size of football fields, people waving tickets at her, asking her if she liked comedy, no safe way to clutch her purse and still drag her bag, the jostling and bumping, people looking at her, Lewis disappearing between two people ahead, that way cinching shut, have to jump the curb, hurrying down a street closed off to cars, a cop on a clomping and snorting horse, where did he go?

And Lewis, meanwhile, darting merrily through the crowd, oblivious to her fears, looking up at the flashing billboard of a practically nude woman illuminated with countless lights, his mouth hanging open like he'd passed out drunk on the recliner.

The green hat, Darnell told herself.

Don't lose it.

The green hat.

It bobbed on a sea of the dead, on a crowd of a different kind.

Darnell could see it rise up in the distance, then slink out of sight. It had been knocked askew during the last day or two. She didn't think it would stay on much longer, wondered if the sticker was still there, that hologram of authenticity.

She followed numbly, but it wasn't Lewis she seemed to be after. Her limbs lurched of their own accord, an unknown number of days passing, losing sight of him and then regaining it.

That green hat.

Darnell didn't heart anything about New York. Not now, not even before this nightmare. She knew something like this would happen. As the sun gradually rose on another day of being trapped, of unholy horror, she felt resigned to never seeing home again. She would have woken up by now if this were a dream. She had given up on thinking this hell wasn't real.

The sun rose and lit the faces of impossibly tall buildings, but not her. Not yet. Darnell was thankful for the night, for the cold that reminded her of Alaska. The smell lessened at night, the shuffle of the mob seemed to slow, the hunger abated. And while there was no sleep, time seemed to pass in long jerks of unconsciousness.

Her prayers had changed over the course of days. At first, she had prayed for it to end, to wake up in that filthy and cramped hotel they'd paid too much for, or to wake up in her home or on a plane. Later, she'd prayed for her soul to go away, for it to leak out her nose or ears and drift up to heaven, to fly away from all the bad her body had done. Now she simply prayed for the cool nighttime, the numbness, the brief interludes of not knowing where she was, what she was doing.

She prayed for the snow.

She thought it would be colder in October in New York, but it had been warm everywhere. A warm year. Not much snow, even back home. And snow made everything look whole. It was the flesh of the soil, the epidermis of Alaska. It turned brown like decay in the sun. But there was no snow in New York City. No flesh. No gleaming white skin to cover the asphalt bones, the gristle in the gutters, the stained underbelly of Manhattan. All that remained was the rot, the putrid browns and the ash charcoals of an Alaskan thaw. And a green hat floating on it like a patch of kelp in Coal Bay, a spot of life among the dead, a remembrance of hope, a symbol of her sorrow, something to pretend she was following.

Anything. Anything but the scent of the terrified and hidden living, clinging to the dark corners for one more day, watching with hope that same sunrise Darnell Lippman sensed with utter dread, a day of hoping not to be eaten, a day of dreading to be fed.

39 ❖ Lewis Lippman

The fat lay in golden layers beneath the skin. It was like roe, stored away amid the deep organs and the bright muscle. The color of butter and the texture of firm cottage cheese, it came away easily and went down hungrily.

Lewis pawed into the woman's steaming abdomen. He made happy, wet smacking sounds and slurped raw fat down his throat. It was as glorious as it was vile. He ate and ate, squishy fists of the stuff oozing through his fingers, his belly straining against a belt he couldn't command his hands to loosen, his distended flesh pinched tight against his blue jeans like a bloated fish that'd been pulled behind his boat for miles.

His bladder and bowels released while he ate. They went at the same time to make more room—and his blue jeans, already caked to his skin, filled with gore. He felt all this, tasted all this. He knelt over the morbidly obese woman they'd caught running through the streets, screaming her fool head off, and he made her fat his fat.

And as Lewis Lippman wallowed in the woman's meat, slurping her golden goodness, he thought about how he'd always hated fat people. And now, how he couldn't get enough.

It was a matter of will, he'd always thought. He hated them for that, for being weak. Why couldn't they just *stop?*

Lewis remembered giving them dirty looks in the marina. He would fire up a cigarette and glare at the waddling tourists who tottered down a finger pier into one of the whale-spotting boats. The docks would groan and shift on Styrofoam floats as they went.

He even said something once in the Chinese restaurant where he and the boys often went for the lunch buffet. He watched as a man well over three hundred pounds grabbed his dirty plate, squeezed out of the booth, and went to attack his seconds or thirds.

"Don'tcha think you've had enough?" he grumbled, just loud enough for the man and his fat family to hear. Kyle and the others laughed, even though Kyle was lugging around a few extra pounds himself. But nothing gross, not like this.

Flashing back to the gruesome present, Lewis watched himself as he dug sideways under the woman's skin. Here was that feller from the buffet that day. No telling them apart from their insides like this. He scooped the fat with his hands, tearing it away from the skin and the meat below, like cleaning a fish.

Lewis used to shock the tourists he took out in his boat by cutting off a piece of a fresh catch and popping it in his mouth. He'd offer them a chunk on the end of his fillet knife and take pleasure in the way they recoiled from him. Once they were out on the sea with him and Kyle, they were stuck. Hauling in the fish they'd dreamed of catching—that they'd paid good money to catch—Lewis would watch them as the seas picked up and they turned a hundred shades of green. He'd delight in their sickness, watch them turn up their noses to the smell when the belly of a nice big jack was opened like a purse, his knife the zipper, the ripe contents sliding toward feet picked off the deck in a hurry.

It was fun, that, having them trapped out there, the sea roiling the lunches in their landlubbing guts, the smell of fish innards that Lewis had become inured to crowding their noses with a ripe stench. He and the others would turn and smile as their fares lost it over the gunwale. Crowds of little fish would come to the surface and chew the lost breakfasts of strangers from Montana, Idaho, and the Dakotas.

And now Lewis was the passenger, the one shitting himself at sea, this concrete sea. A world he'd dreamed of seeing, that he'd fantasized about from a distance, Times Square with all those crowds as the ball dropped, as the date changed for the East Coast well ahead of the great big nothing that happened in Coal Bay.

He was the tourist, now. He was trapped in this skull of his, watching the guts spill, smelling the horror, feeling sick and being unable to vomit. He was the man growing bloated like a fish dragged on the end of a line, the man with his plate, bending over seconds and thirds. No willpower. No willpower in the world was enough.

Lewis tried to remember days on the docks, smoking cigarettes, watching fat tourists from the Dakotas bend the finger piers as they crowded onto whale-spotting boats. He tried to remember it again without him glaring, without the sneers and jokes to Kyle and the others. In his mind, he took another glorious drag from that smoke before flicking it into the sea with a sputtering hiss. He tried to travel back there, to pretend the little globules of yellow fat sucked out of his palms were caviar and that the rats burrowing in among his knees to feed alongside him were little fish, nosing up to the surface, eating the chum from the guts of strangers, and that this time he wouldn't turn and smile and judge anymore.

40 ✤ Darnell Lippman

D arnell had hoped and prayed from the moment she was attacked that someone would come for her. But not like this. This wasn't a rescue. It was the hand of some angry god reaching down from the clouds and plucking her off the ground. She was discarded fruit, all of them were. Nasty fruit fallen from a tree and riddled with worms, and now they have come to choose the rotten among the rotten.

They lured them into their trap with blood. Blood and something else. Darnell thought of her husband chumming for sharks off Spit Point. She knew what these people were doing, and still it worked. It was like that cartoon she'd clipped for Lewis, the one with a fish commenting on a hook before going for the bait. It knew, and still it went. It had no choice. There was only the hunger.

This wasn't the first trap they'd set. She'd seen them try before, the helicopters swooping in among the same low buildings, the same alleys. Whatever they'd used the first time didn't work. The smell wasn't right. Darnell wondered if it was animal blood at first, or human blood with the life melted out of it, maybe with the soul evaporated. That first time, she could smell the copper in the air, but it didn't move her feet. It wasn't the same.

They came back the next day with something different; her group could smell it. Their shuffling went from aimless to concerted action as they spilled into the baited alley, the *thwump-thwump-thwump* of the fishermen hovering in helicopters overhead, a rotor like an outboard, the hook both visible and irresistible.

Darnell and the others bit. The alley tightened between a set of rusty green dumpsters. She was near the front, crowding against the pawing others, the groans and grunts filling the narrow space between the buildings with an eerie roar. One of the dumpsters squealed as the crush of undead pressed hard enough to jar its wheels. Those alongside her kicked through trash, waving their arms after the fetid odor, a long rope like a line with a sinker and bobber dangling down between the brick walls.

They could see it. Darnell knew everyone else could see the lure as well. And still, they went after.

The alley forked where it met the crumbling wall of the building along its back. The sun was low, the shadows deep, and the smell was everywhere. It trailed off in both directions, further dividing the narrow stream of disfigured and disgusting animals.

Darnell was being culled from the herd. She felt the panic of a hook sinking into her lip, the lonely fear of being left to drown. Where was Lewis? She wept silently and tearlessly, powerfully alone, wishing he were there, but she hadn't seen his hat for days.

She hurried at the front of the group that veered left, following the smell of blood and the smell of something else as well. It was a heady odor she'd nosed from a man with a split skull, a feed from a week ago. The smell of brains.

Onward, deeper into the alley, *thwump-thwump-thwump* from the propeller above her. Darnell imagined it was Lewis. He was here to catch her, to lift her out of her misery and into his reeking boat, to wrap her in a blanket and tell her that he loved her, to make her feel safe.

She and three others were standing on the net when it rose up from the camouflage of newspapers and soggy cardboard. The man beside her with the broken leg was caught on the edge. As the net cinched tight, he tumbled out, his foot catching in one of the square holes, grunts from the rest of them as they were pressed together and lifted skyward.

The man with the broken leg wiggled free and tumbled with a sick crunch to the pavement. Darnell and the other two were packed gill to gill in the tight net. There was a sinking feeling in her stomach as they rose higher. The man beside her made a gurgling sound. He was chewing the rope, the air so laden with the scent of blood and brains that Darnell feared one of the monsters would begin to chew on her. Or that she might turn on them.

Fortunately, she was too pinned to do so. Instead, she watched through a hole in the net as the rooftops of the low buildings came into view and as the helicopter pulled them up into the low rays of the setting sun. The city below seemed to shrink. The cars scattered everywhere became toys, the people moving amongst them like clumsy insects. The totality of the horror loomed below, smoke drifting from fires, a bus turned on its side, something moving within. The helicopter angled out over one of the rivers that framed the city on either side—Darnell didn't know their names, couldn't tell which direction they were flying. The net drifted behind on its long strand of cable, the air numbingly cold. She saw a bridge she recognized from postcards, the stone arches like something on a church. It was a landmark, a distinctly New York monument, and it was in ruin. The center half was gone, tangles of broad cables dangling toward the icy waters, piers of pavement laced with iron bars that jutted out like mangled limbs.

The two other bridges she could see were the same, the middles blown to bits. The island had been cast off. Darnell thought of all the mornings she'd brought coffee down to the dock, chatted with Lewis while he'd loaded the boat, then tossed him his lines. She would stand there, watching him chug out toward the inlet, her hands smelling like the fishy ropes, the steam dissipating from her rapidly cooling mug.

The net spun lazily beneath the helicopter, the earth seeming to revolve on its axis below. One of the creatures pinned beside her gnawed on her arm, the scent of blood still in the net. Darnell could feel the bites but could not move. She watched, frozen and numb in more ways than one, as a loathsome spit of land drifted away, and knew that this time her fears would be confirmed. Darnell Lippman knew she would never see her husband again.

41 ❖ Lewis Lippman

Healing was the strangest of things. His stricken condition gave Lewis time to ponder the basic stuff, stuff you never thought about. Like healing. When you got down to it, healing was far stranger than what he did now. What he was doing now seemed natural. *This* was how things should be. Not because it was better or preferable, but because it just made more sense.

There was a gash on Lewis's forearm from swimming through a pile of wrecked cars to get at a survivor. And now, with his hands out in front of him as he staggered along, he was able to study the wound, able to see the white bone where it lay exposed between the torn flesh. Strands of what he thought was muscle hung out in cables and ropes. It was like the insides of every fish he'd caught, but it was him. And this made more sense, that things were cut and they stayed cut. How much stranger was the notion that they could knit back together, that wounds could disappear?

It was like those lizards that lost their tails and grew them back. These were mutant abilities taken for granted, abilities no less strange than the closing of a nick. His friend Kyle had that scar on his leg from his long-lining days, that nasty length of white tissue bumped up along his knee from where the hook got him and wouldn't let go. How was that normal, a body knowing what part of itself it was supposed to be? Knowing how to grow across and stitch to its neighbor, and then knowing when to stop? He knew people who had complained about their scars, about this miraculous gift. It never occurred to them that their wound could just as easily hang open.

There was a white cord of tendon dangling from Lewis's arm, and this was how things were meant to be. A man would be careful if he knew ahead of time that wounds didn't grow back. People would act different, think twice. No more bumbling about with arms flailing, not looking where they were going.

Lewis rarely looked where he was going. He tried to remember the first time he'd yelled at his wife. It'd been back before they'd gotten married, but just a time or two. Hadn't really lit into her until later. There was the time she'd wrecked the truck, said it was a patch of black ice, but he'd let her have it anyway. Never struck her, but she recoiled just the same. Made him feel like shit, the way she flinched from his words. Pissed him off even more for her to make him feel that way.

"It's just a scratch," she'd tried to tell him.

A scratch. In a thing that don't heal, he could see that now. Another scratch, and the wound is open. Emotions don't know how to stitch back the way flesh could. How do you go to a person, your wife of two decades, and tell her you want to start over again? How do you say, "Forget everything we've got together. Forget the kids and the fights and all the good times, too. I take it all back." How do you do that? It ain't a lizard's tail, those years. It ain't something you walk away from and start over.

A gash is what it becomes. And then a stump, until you can't feel it anymore. Until there's just an itch where things used to be, a phantom love you feel silly for recalling. Now it's someone who takes care of the kids, does the dishes, talks your head off when you get back from being on the water a few days. Now it's just someone you live with. It's excuses to get away so you can meet the boys at the bar. It's inconvenient phone calls in the winter when she's visiting her sister in Anchorage, too scared to walk out of the grocery store and across the parking lot in the dark. That was a wound, that one. Yelling at her for being afraid. Yelling at her to keep up all the time. Yelling at her for being scared of the crowds in the city.

Goddamn, he missed her. Why didn't he ever tell her that? Those long nights on the water with the decks slippery and lit up from the flood lights, Kyle telling a joke, and all Lewis wanted was to get home to a hot meal, to their bed, to a hug and her joking that if his neck smelled any more like fish he'd have gills.

And he'd feel it for a little while, that joy of being home, but never say it. Little cells of thought that didn't know how to reach out to the other side and start pulling back together. A tongue for lashing but not for stitching.

He missed her terribly now that he felt this fear of the crowd, the helplessness that she must've felt. And he had yelled at her for it, for being afraid. All he'd had to say was that it was gonna be okay, but he'd made it worse instead. It was easier to imagine, now, how the world must've seemed to her. The fear of not being in control. The fear of being lost all the time. Lewis no longer had any idea where he was—all the blocks looked the same to him. He had no map, no chart, no points of reference. The first time he'd popped up from a subway station, back before all the madness began, he'd felt the first tickle of this, of not knowing where he was. You pop up and you can't see the horizon. Just tall buildings on all sides, no feeling of where east or west was, no idea which way to start out, all turned around from winding down a flight of stairs in one part of the city, riding that train somewhere, and then winding his way back up. Dizzy, and he couldn't ask anyone, couldn't do that, not in front of her. It was scary, feeling that for the first time. Completely and utterly lost.

Darnell must've felt like that a lot.

It was getting colder every day, and Lewis wondered if the pain would eventually get so great that he wouldn't feel anything anymore. Enough wounds, and you just go numb. He hoped that happened soon. He was just glad it wasn't August with all that heat. The smell and the torture would be worse in August. Maybe he would still be alive and around then and he'd find out. But he hoped not. He'd rather be buried in the snow come winter, cover these wounds up. That was the thing about a scratch or a gash: sometimes there weren't no healing from them at all. Sometimes you had to hope for them to get worse and worse until the mechanisms shut down, until you couldn't feel nothing. That was easier, somehow. Easier than doing the unnatural thing—than doing whatever it took to stitch a wound back to how it was before.

42 ❖ Darnell Lippman

She thought the helicopter would take them far away, would whisk them out over the river to the forest of low buildings and those red-and-white factory smokestacks beyond. But the net swayed to the side as the helicopter banked low over the water. And pinned to the rough twine of the net, a man chewing on her arm, the scent of blood in the cool air, Darnell peered through the holes of her confinement and spotted the thing they were aiming for.

It was a pair of barges strapped together, the kind that pushed through Homer Sound with tugs chugging at their stern. Orange rust, like lacy adornment, decorated the barges. Taut cables stretched from the corners of their metal decks out to the rock-shrouded legs of one of the ruined bridges. The river flowed angrily against the contraption, upset at this intrusion along its surface. On one side, the water pushed and frothed in a white mustache. Eddies and curls of water danced and spun along the calmer side, the river racing and turbulent and chilly.

They drifted down toward the combined decks of the two barges, and Darnell saw the small sheds dotting their surface. They looked like the containers from ships, the backs of tractor trailers, or those little temporary classrooms the middle school bought because it couldn't afford anything else. Plastic tubes ran between the containers, the wind from the props causing them to shimmer and whip about. It was a hastily constructed place, this metal island set in the roiling waters. A good sign, Darnell thought. The ruined bridges and this rusted place were good signs. They didn't want the horror to spread, which maybe meant that it hadn't.

Her thoughts drifted to one of Lewis's favorite TV shows as the helicopter made its slow descent. It was a show about the men and women who worked border control down south, a terribly long way from Alaska. She remembered how those men would round up people at night with goggles that turned the world green, that made eyeballs shine like headlamps in the tall grass. They rounded them up and treated them something like this, something less than human but not quite animal.

She remembered dark-skinned immigrants with plastic straps around their wrists. They were shoved into vans by men with guns so big they rested them on their shoulders. These men chewed toothpicks and wore shades and smiled and talked into the cameras. Lewis loved these men, even though they lived and worked a terribly long way from Alaska. "Keeping the country clean," he'd said, finishing another beer and crushing the tin with his fist.

The net of writhing monsters landed harshly on the wet and rusty decks, right beside a large white 'H' painted in the middle of a big circle. Darnell couldn't feel her own skin from the frigid ride, couldn't tell if the man pinned beside her was still biting her arm or not.

People in plastic suits came at them warily with long poles and hooks. They tugged the nets loose with these tools, and the helicopter made thwumping sounds as the rotor kept spinning. A man in a shiny helmet peered through the helicopter's window toward the net, gloved hand on the glass. As soon as they got the net free, the rotor grew more angry, and the helicopter lifted away.

Darnell's nose was frozen stiff, and the men with the poles were completely covered, but she could still catch a faint whiff of the living on them. Her ghastly neighbors could, too. Their ragged breath fogged the air with hungry grunts. Darnell suspected something different was wrong with these other two, that the locals, the New Yorkers who'd gotten sick, had lost their minds more fully. It never occurred to her that they were as trapped as she, or that any of them might be tourists as well, or that her breath was also clouding the air and filling it with inhuman sounds. In her mind, it was just she who was out of place and alone. Everyone else was different.

The men in the suits sure treated them the same. They used poles like for wrangling rabid dogs and hooked their limbs. One suited figure snagged Darnell's wrist, another dropped a loop around her neck. She watched as they tried to snare the arm of her neighbor, but he had no hand to catch it on, so the loop kept sliding off his black and mangled wrist. Muffled shouts and pointing from the men in the yellow suits, and they managed to tighten the loop over his elbow.

The three of them were half-dragged across the steel deck, slippery with sea salt and ice. Darnell's feet tangled in the net imbued with someone's blood and brains. She fought against these men, but not of her own accord. She was precisely the animal they were treating her like.

Darnell remembered being *not sick*. She wanted to tell them, tell them she remembered being petrified that she might catch it, holding her breath, cowering in a department store, wondering where Lewis had gotten to, why he wasn't answering his cell phone. This wasn't her. She wasn't like this.

Any slack in the poles, and her long gray fingernails swiped at their masked faces, an inhuman power wrestling against the sticks, a croak of a scream dribbling out. They pulled her through an inflated arch and into one of the trailers, one not connected to the rest. Loud fans whirred, more cool air on thawing flesh, the tingle of frost-nipped skin, the half-numb of an Alaskan night spent camping out too early—too eagerly—in the spring. Darnell snapped at one of the men in the suits. This was not like her at all.

Glass rooms for each of them. More rooms in the trailer as well, but all empty. They were the first. There were drains in the floor, gurneys with straps, chains bolted to the walls with metal plates. The men held Darnell with their sticks and loops of wire, the one around her neck causing her to gurgle, the pain very real as her flesh thawed.

She was pinned against the wall, the skin of the trailer booming as her elbow slammed into it with animal strength. One of the men, visor fogged with effort or nerves, stepped forward and secured her ankle with a pole. As she snapped at him, she saw that her net-mates were getting similar treatment beyond the glass. All the workers pulled, lifting her into the air, a fresh catch flopping on the end of a line. It felt like they would rip her body apart, pulling her in all directions like that. She was moved over the gurney, hovered there, and then was settled down. Cool against her back. Each limb was pinned with the sticks until they could work the straps tight. Darnell wrestled against the pinch on her wrists and ankles. If she had a pulse—she wasn't sure if she did or didn't—surely it would be cut off. The straps were too tight.

They released her and withdrew their poles, and Darnell bucked against her restraints. She was a monster in a film, a horrible movie, her view through the screen the wrong way.

A groan leaked out as she tried to form the words. She really concentrated this time, did her best to yell out that she was a person inside there, that she was a real person and not an animal. She wasn't like the others caught in the net with her; she was different, still alive.

She tried to form these words, but they remained loud thoughts. Silent screams. All that emerged were roars and spit. She arched her back and banged on the gurney just like the monsters in the other rooms, but she wasn't like them. Images from a TV show her husband used to watch flooded back. She wasn't like these people at all.

43 ❖ Lewis Lippman

ewis was lost. He had no idea what street he was on or which part of town he was in. But he knew he'd finally found what they were all looking for, the source of this alluring odor drifting through the air: It was meat, holed up in the middle of a massive intersection the size of a city block. The smell oozed through and over a barrier wall of cars and trucks, tantalizing but nearly drowned out as he got closer by the reek of the undead pressed all around. There was a bus, one of the big flat-fronted kind that rose high as an overpass and brought whale-watchers from Anchorage. It had been parked sideways, nose crushed against an old brick facade, a dump truck shoved against its rear.

Lewis's group melded with the many others that were already there, a fucking jamboree of zombies. They all milled around, groaning like a bunch of drunks, like goddamn stoned hippies waiting for a show to start. They crowded at each other's backs, all hoping to be near the stage.

Lewis rode a surge through the crowd. A woman pressed against him, her lower jaw missing, tongue dangling down like a necktie, eyes wide with fear. Her gurgles had a unique ring to them. She disappeared, replaced by the sight of a tall man who must've been one of the first to go. A patch of hair on his scalp and ribbons of flesh stretched across his cheek were almost all that remained on his skull. His eyes were comically wide, much too round. Maggots the size of peanuts dotted his neck.

So many stages of decay, so many people, but not people anymore. Lewis was pushed forward by the crowds at his back. Some of those ahead were shambling the other direction as if disappointed the show wouldn't start. It was hard to smell the living meat from the middle of the crowd; the change in scents created eddies of undead, a swirling of rotting bodies like by the fish cleaning station at slack tide.

Lewis made it to the front and found himself pressed against the bus. There were smears there from those who came before, a clump of hair and a bit of flesh. He felt something like a gag reflex in his mind, but his body made no response. It was searching after the smell of meat.

Gunshots rang out from above. He had heard potshots the day before as he closed in on the area, wondered what they were shooting at. If anyone in the crowd took a hit, he couldn't see. There were others at his back trying to take his place, and Lewis found himself shoved to the side along the length of the bus. He could imagine himself swirling like this forever until he looked like the man with the maggots on his neck. Another shot from what sounded like a high caliber rifle. That was another possibility, another way out. He tried to gurgle louder, to make himself a target, to seem especially threatening. He thought of a movie he'd seen once with monsters like him in it, had laughed while they trudged forward in a stupor getting their heads blown off, and now it occurred to him that maybe they were begging for it. Maybe they were trying to hold perfectly still.

Stupid thoughts. Just a movie. Actors. They hadn't been thinking shit other than when the next smoke break was coming or hitting those tables of food. Fuck, Lewis couldn't stop thinking about food and cigarettes. He banged his knee on something, something hard. One of those luggage compartments had come open, had been knocked loose.

There was a smell. Lewis fell to the ground, sniffing. Others joined him. They could go even closer to the stage, he realized. They could go *under* it.

He crawled inside the compartment, over a cardboard box wrapped in tape and past a duffel bag. A few suitcases crowded a dark corner, the other side of the compartment shut tight.

Lewis banged against it. Others pressed up behind him, knees ringing on steel, heads hitting the roof, dark and cramped and slamming against this other door, wondering if it might pop loose as well.

44 ❖ Darnell Lippman

They left Darnell alone on the gurney with her thoughts. When her head twisted to the side, she could see them working on one of the others in the adjoining room. They crowded around while the monster thrashed, back arching and knees kicking, men in rubber suits trying to hold it still while doctors went to work.

She didn't see it all. Her eyes roamed, following the smells coming through the loose joints and cracks of the place. It looked hastily put together. It reminded her of Lewis's boat with its rough scars of metal where he used those bright torches to join plates together. The glass was glued in with something like that 5200 stuff. She knew from the clothes he ruined. "What's this?" She would scratch at the hardened crust on his bluejeans. "Fifty-two hundred," he'd say. Always 5200. Funny the things she remembered.

The barge didn't sway much, not that she could tell. It was pinned by those taut cables and the stiff current. It had to be a good sign, this quarantine. They were trying. There were people out there trying something. The non-infected were doing more than running away or fighting back. And the bridges, that had to be good, too. Darnell thought so. There were so many others to think about. The kids, her parents, all her friends back home. They would be watching TV and calling the authorities, letting them know she and Lewis were in the city, that their cell phones were going straight to voice mail, that they needed help.

Help is here, Darnell thought. *Help is coming.*

They finished what they were doing to the monster in the next room, and then they came for her, five of them in yellow rubber suits, the same material as Lewis's knee-high fishing boots. They had hoods built into the suits with plastic visors the size of lunchboxes. Two men with wrinkled brows stood over her and held her shoulders. Darnell felt herself lunge after them, teeth clacking, and she wanted to apologize for this behavior the way her sister was forever apologizing for her yipping dogs. "It isn't their fault," Gladys would say. "They're just being dogs."

An older woman leaned over, wisps of gray hair framing a face of concentration or worry, hard to tell which. She had old eyes with crow's feet at the corners and directed the others, her voice muffled by the plastic but her lips moving. She pointed with her thick gloves while machines were arranged, more tools laid out. Darnell's body twisted and strained against the straps pinning her into place. It was as if the monster side of her knew better than she did what was about to happen. It was as if it were more afraid than she.

They tightened the straps to keep her from yanking about. She could barely move. It felt wonderful to be pinned perfectly still like that—her limbs could no longer betray her. They would see, now that she was calm, they would see in her eyes that she was okay, that she was more terrified than they were.

Her clothes were cut off, nasty scraps of fabric peeled away and preserved like they were unwrapping a gosh-darned mummy. Swabs on her skin, placed into baggies. A long stick shoved between her teeth and her gums, bagged up as well.

Yes, take your samples, Darnell thought. *Make me better.*

She was thinking this as the swabs and the wooden sticks were put away. A black bundle was placed on the steel table. Plastic canisters like Tupperware were arranged. Someone began to draw on her, began to probe her skin and tap on her chest with stiffened fingers. Darnell pleaded with her eyes—she tried to let them know she was in there. She tried to speak, all to no avail.

The bundle was unrolled. It reminded her of her mother's silverware. And then the implements were removed, one by one, and placed on the table. Curved things that gleamed in the overhead light. Tiny and sharp things. Something like pliers. Alien tools. Expensive tools.

The old woman with the kind and wrinkled eyes held out a gloved hand. Her lips moved, and a tiny blade was placed handle-first into her palm. Darnell gurgled and tried to form the words. She wanted to cry, but felt nothing on her cheeks. In the next room, a monster rattled its chains behind the glass.

Please, Darnell thought as the blade was brought to her stomach. *Don't.*

There was a dull ache as the woman went to work. Not the sharp sting of a little cut, but the deep bruise of something much worse. One of the men by the table of tools turned and looked away. The other reached forward with the little canister like something used for leftovers while the woman with the wrinkled eyes took her sample. A pinch. The smell of rotten blood. Another sample—Darnell in agony—but no closer to death, as they removed her flesh piece by gory piece.

They aren't here to save me, she realized. *Dear God, they're seeing what it takes to kill me.*

45 ❖ Lewis Lippman

It was loud in the compartment. Not just the constant banging of knees and elbows, but the grunts and groans from those pressed in beside him. Lewis hit his head repeatedly on the metal arms that held the door shut from the inside. His hands slapped uselessly against the wall. But it was someone else that broke the door free. Just the right spasm with their hand, and suddenly a crack of light appeared at Lewis's knees. The dark barrier in front of him hinged up, swung away, and vile humans swarmed out like dirty rats.

There was a cry of alarm, someone screaming, gunshots. Bodies tumbled over Lewis and crawled forward. They stood and lurched toward the men and women scrambling everywhere. They fell down when shot or just spun around and kept going. Lewis tried to stand and kept getting knocked back down. So many. Like oil spilling through a funnel, coming and coming. The gunshots were like fireworks, *pow pow pow*. The smell of meat, human and something else. Something cooking. Dogs or birds, who knew? Chaos. An encampment of cars.

The cars were like tents, people moving inside, more running from a clearing in the middle of the intersection to dive into open vehicles and slam the doors shut. Windows were cracked, barrels poking out. Their aim wasn't good. Lewis saw one of his kind break out the back glass of a yellow cab and begin to worm her way inside. Her dress caught and tore on the bumper. She was shot in the head and fell limp, but there were more to follow. People were shouting about the bus, trying to organize, but it was every man for himself. The undead swarmed, spilling and spilling through.

Lewis banged on the side of a car, trying to get at the meat inside. A pistol, a small black thing, waved in his face. The muzzle flashed like a camera, the taste of powder in his mouth, a punch to his teeth. Lewis spun around as another shot went off, the zing of a far ricochet. Another zombie reached her fingers in the window, a young girl, a teen. She broke the top half of the glass out just as a bullet went through her brain. Collapsing, her arms twitched against Lewis's shins as he reached through the hole she'd made. A bullet slammed into his shoulder, a last gasp from the young man inside, and then Lewis had a hold of him, others had a hold of him, dragged him out into the streets.

Gunfire grew heavy, and then lessened. There was a pause for reloading, a last round of patter, and then the relative quiet as a boisterous family finally sat down to eat. The feed became an orgy. Fights broke out over the scraps, a man still able to scream as his arms and legs went different directions, lungs bellowing even as ropes of purple intestines were pulled away like a magician's scarf.

Lewis spun in the middle of it all, eating and terrified, wounds throbbing, the muted pops of gunfire fading into the distance, the sudden appearance of a helicopter several blocks away, doing nothing, watching, drawn perhaps to the noise of this last stand, this party, the fireworks and celebration of no one's independence.

46 ❖ Darnell Lippman

The woman in the suit was clinical and calm as she went about her sample-taking. It didn't matter that Darnell felt alive, she was cut into like a cadaver, like a swollen thing washed up on the rocks. The straps kept her pinned to the table, muscles straining futilely. She tried to scream as the knife bit into her, but the cry for help stayed with the agony, locked up inside her head, hers alone to hear and endure.

The doctor rarely looked Darnell in the face as she worked. Her exhalations fogged the plastic visor of her suit, and her voice remained a muted drone. But when her lips moved, the men behind her reacted. Some kind of radio, like on Lewis's boat, like the handheld he kept by the recliner in case a fishing buddy got into trouble. Darnell imagined squeezing that radio and calling for help, calling for Lewis to come and get her. She was awash in misery, drowning, stranded, bit at by gleaming fish that carried away her flesh. And the worst part was that she couldn't die.

Her twitching muscles felt near enough like wracking sobs. Struggling on that table felt near enough like times she'd clutched her knees and sobbed quietly in the tub. Life and love. When the bad parts crept in, sometimes she wished it would end. Wished there was some quick way out for cowards. She loved her husband, wasn't sure how not to, but sometimes she sat in the tub with the water running dangerously hot and wanted out. Like now, just wanting to die.

The doctor took something from her abdomen without asking. Machines beeped and whirred as they measured the nothing. But there was still something there, something they couldn't take. And the struggles against those straps felt near enough like uncontrolled sobs.

Darnell opened her eyes, couldn't remember closing them, wasn't sure how. But the dry and burning in them that she had long grown used to was gone for a moment, something like a spider's touch tickling her rotting cheeks. And above her, a fogged visor cleared as the old woman with wrinkled eyes held her breath, watching, squinting, staring through Darnell's eyes and deep into whatever remained of her soul.

Darnell lunged forward with her thoughts, her prayers, her begging wishes. She felt her arms and legs strain against the straps. She screamed and screamed as loud as she could, yelling "HEY!" and "HELP!" and "I'M ALIVE!"

The woman in the puffy suit remained frozen. After a pause, her lips moved. The men by the tables stirred, hard to see what they were doing. The doctor held Darnell's gaze a moment longer, then pulled away, the flash of a blade disappearing, the torment coming to an end.

Darnell was left in motionless agony. All her new wounds sang to her. They were electric currents clipped to her naked flesh, the juice dialed up and down, up and down, sagging and spiking. She lay there for what felt like days. When her head lolled to the side, she could see the man in the next cage bucking against his straps, no one else around.

The people in the puffy suits returned. A bright light stabbed Darnell in the eyes. The man holding her head wore metal gloves of a fine mesh that reminded Darnell of Lewis cleaning his fish. Lewis sometimes wore gloves like that.

Her head was strapped still. She had the sense that things would soon get worse, not better. More probes were stuck to her flesh, itching. Equipment set up. Something by her head, a heavy box, scraping against the metal surface of the table.

The doctor held a wire, a thin cord. She bent it into a gentle curve, tapped her finger on the end and there was a harsh pop from the box. She did this again: *tap, tap. Pop, pop.*

Darnell could smell oil on the metal glove as the man forced her chin down, as he held her mouth open. The doctor's lips were moving. She slid the cord into Darnell's mouth, across her tongue, into her throat. The box, the speaker by her head, amplified the grunts and rattling groans. Darnell was horrified by the sound of what she'd become. It was like a mirror turned on a burn victim.

She cried out, and the speaker hissed with her pointless breath. Darnell wondered how long it could go on, how many ways they could experiment on her, when her affliction would finally end. The woman with the kind eyes watched her, waiting, measuring something. Darnell had no idea. They all seemed to be waiting. Expecting. What had they seen? They were looking at her differently, now. Like they wondered if someone was peering back.

"I'M HERE!" Darnell yelled. She screamed with that voice that appeared when she read, when she thought to herself, that silent voice that somehow could be heard, could have an accent, could be quiet or loud, but always silent.

"HELP!" she cried. "HELP HELP HELP HELP."

She threw the words over and over, pounded them like her pulse forgotten, made that reading voice a wispy rattle in her neck, audible in her cheeks, deafening in her skull.

"I'M ALIVE! I'M ALIVE! I'M IN HERE! HELP! HELP! HELP!"

The speaker gurgled with wet sounds. Something was adjusted. The doctors leaned close as if they heard a whisper. Darnell could only hear her pleading screams in her head and the amplified, bodily noises her thrashing made.

HELP HELP HELP.

There came a trickle of tears from her exertion. Wrinkles faded as eyes widened. And Darnell felt the strangeness of a connection, of a person reacting to her thoughts, the thrill of communication. Her chest and neck felt sore from trying so hard to scream, it coming out no more than a hissing whisper. But it was enough. The cord was extracted. The doctor stood. Equipment was gathered, and once again, Darnell was left alone for what felt an eternity.

••••

They returned with a roll of paper, a gently curving line etched down the middle, nearly flat, something from one of their useless machines. It was just paper, now, something to write on. That's all it would ever be.

With a fat black marker, the same kind they'd used to draw on her flesh before cutting it, something was written:

1 for Yes. 2 for No.

Darnell felt a flush of hope. The wire slid back into her mouth, as welcome as that suction tube from the dentist. More writing.

Can you read this?

Darnell tried to blink, but couldn't. She screamed YES in her mind, felt like she could hear it in her cheeks. She yelled ONE. She yelled YES YES YES, and heard mostly gurgles. The doctor seemed agitated, anxious. Darnell worried she should have only tried yelling a single word. Maybe that's what they were after. A length of paper was torn off. The doctor tried tossing it to the side, but it stuck to her rubber gloves. One of the men helped her. She pressed the marker back to the roll with that gentle, wavy line.

Is there anyone in there?

Darnell imagined taking a deep breath. It was more a pause of thought. She gathered her will, all her imagined strength, and tried to force it out all at once, to erupt in a mighty roar, all the screams she'd ever felt inside while sitting in her tub, clutching her shins, trying not to let Lewis hear her cry:

YEEEEESSSSS

There was a moment of stillness, a place that heartbeats used to fill. The other doctors came into view as they crowded around, as they bent over to peer at her. The marker squeaked against the glossy paper.

We want to help you.

Darnell felt a wave of anger rather than relief. Parts of her were missing, were sitting in plastic tubs and containers. Her wounds, the damage to her flesh, could still be felt. She felt exhausted from the effort of crying out. Her chest was empty in more ways than one. She was exhausted from the long death she was suffering, but Darnell summoned the last of her will.

KILL! she yelled, sensing that these people could hear, that the screams in her head were quiet words that leaked out their box and into the room; they emanated like some pale echo deep in her throat.

KILL ME! DIE DIE DIE DIE!

Like the gulls by the pier while Lewis cleaned fish:

DIE DIE DIE DIE!

The birds floating on the air, swooping for scraps, for flesh torn mindlessly from bone:

KILL KILL KILL KILL!

The doctor straightened. Darnell collapsed within herself, her consciousness drained, the animal within her taking over her limbs again, writhing against the bonds while doctors in puffy suits stood around, lips moving, conferring.

They were going to help her, she thought. Darnell had done it. She had made a connection, had reached out to another human being and made contact. She sobbed without moving, cried without shedding a tear. And when the paper appeared above her with the simple question: **You wish you were dead?** she could do little more than emit a soft gurgle, a dry croak, a whisper from her sturdy tomb.

The room fell deathly quiet. The cord was removed from her throat, the speaker scratching the table as it was pulled away, the little wires and itchy cups pulled from her skin, and Darnell thought they were going to do it, right then, somehow. She prayed they would bring mercy on her, that they would bring mercy upon them all.

47 ❖ Lewis Lippman

A gray dawn broke over the destroyed encampment. Falling from the sky was what Kyle liked to call a "fighting snow." It was those fat flakes that came down the size of silver dollars and laden with moisture. Lewis had seen them get palm-sized back home, even as big around as dinner plates. When a few inches of these flakes gathered, you could scoop up a snowball in your hand, give it a squeeze, and hurl away. With enough work, you could compress it down to a ball of ice that'd leave a bruise or dent a car.

It must've been snowing at night for so much to accumulate. Lewis hadn't felt a thing. His skin was too numb to know anything was coming down at all. He did hear some crunching when he came to now and then, as he circled within the walls that had trapped the living. But in his groggy half-sleep he had figured the sound for more of the broken glass that littered the scene of yesterday's fight.

It almost made him feel home again, seeing the snow as the sky brightened. It was the sort of day he loved to spend on the water, those early morning hours when the sea was flat as glass, when the only breeze was the one he made with the throttle, and when the sun didn't rise so much as the clouds lightened from coal black to ash gray.

Home. Homer, Alaska.

No matter how badly he'd like to be there, Lewis knew he never would again. He was trapped. They were all trapped. High walls of steel, cars jumbled up, buses and dump trucks. There would be no call for stooping down and squeezing out of that block-sized arena. No way to the other side of that hastily constructed fence. Lewis had it worse than those damn Mexicans. All they had to do was scale a wall, crawl through some grass, go for a swim, and they were pretty much free to live wherever they wanted. They weren't pinned like this.

Damn Mexicans.

Lewis couldn't feel his feet. His shoes were soaked and frozen solid, his toes little cubes of ice. He would love to have wept for his feet, which must be ruined. Frostbitten. Falling apart. Probably worse than his arm, which hung open and gathered snow. His flesh was gray, two fingers bent backwards, and all he wanted was to go home. He wanted to see his kids. See Darnell. What the fuck had he done with his life?

Killed a bunch of fish. Made more money than he needed to. He could've stopped going out if he'd spent it smarter. If he'd invested. But it was always there for the taking, just a few nights out with his crew and he'd come back with enough to pay the bank, fill up with diesel, sit at the bar a few nights and check out asses and down beers.

Lewis couldn't feel anything. Not his body. But he felt something else, something besides the regret. He felt sad for the way he used to get a kick out of seeing them Mexicans get rounded up. Goddamn, there was enough fishing out there to do. He made more than he needed. Enough to waste. What he shoulda done is spent more time with his family.

The snow was a few inches deep. Enough to cover the bodies scattered in the streets. Fires were burning out of control in the buildings overhead, survivors overrun by the undead who managed to worm inside. The remnants of this last bastion of humanity were rising in the form of gray smoke, billowing up to touch the sad sky, a stream of ash rising like a river to a broader sea.

The world below, meanwhile, was turning white, getting its skin back. And across the confines of that city block, there shuffled dark and grisly shapes. Blacks, Hispanics, Jews, Asians, who knew what else. They were all starting to look the same to Lewis, anyway. Same deadened skin turning shades of pale gray, same collections of wounds, of gashes and cuts, same tattered clothes and scraps of fashion, just one river of tottering undead with their arms out, mouths open, eyes wide and unblinking, the snow dusting their hair and hiding their hurts.

One mass, Lewis thought. All the damn same. And goddamn, all he wanted was to go home, to be with his family. But he couldn't. There was no river to cross, nothing to crawl through. He was more stuck than birthright, forced to live where his feet were pinned. He thought of all the fish he'd seen flapping on his deck, eyeing the scuppers, no chance in hell of ever getting over the side. He thought of all the times he'd felt that twinge, just a pause, to knock a fish with his boot, to send it back into the water to be with its family, but he never did. He was a man with a knife and metal gloves standing on that deck. And he never did.

Part VI

The Swooping Birds that Caught Her Eyes

48 ❖ Jeffery Biggers

The jets were flying low. They rumbled down the Hudson, booms and echoes like thunderclaps amid the walls of glass and steel, and Jeffery was reminded of that September morning so long ago. He'd been a boy, cutting class because it was too beautiful outside, when he'd heard the roar of the jet overhead, a distant grumble, acrid smoke filling the air for days and days.

Most of the pack ignored the whine of the turbines, but it triggered a deep memory for Jeffery. It was the sound of deployment, the noise of good men and women ferried off to another life. It was stub-nosed C-130s and C-5As that left with children and came home mostly empty. Only the bags were full. Laid out on the deck. All black. The color of grief. Plastic zippered up tight.

His head lifted, some primal fear network still intact, still pulling the puppet's strings. Navy gray slid across the brilliant blue, contrails of speed and the cool atmosphere streaking from wingtips. The lead jet was in a dive. Jeffery remembered jumping out of a plane a long time ago. He remembered thinking the chute wouldn't open, that he would plummet to his death. He remembered calling his mom from camp, still breathless, her so proud of all the places he was going, the things he was doing.

He only told her about the good places. The good things.

The landing gear was open, hatch doors like little fins on the plane's belly, clear as day. Nothing sticking out.

Jeffery remembered flying home—he remembered the party they threw. All his mom's friends had crowded around. They grabbed his biceps and patted his stomach, squealed and told him how handsome he was, showed him their phones, pictures of their daughters.

He had smiled and eaten off his paper plate, standing up, telling himself to eat slow. No mortars would scream into the mess tent. He wouldn't have to drop what he was doing and find his rifle. Smile and eat. A woman twice his age told him how pretty his eyes were. How the military done him good.

He had nodded, didn't tell her what his eyes had seen. Five miles driving a jeep, an arm in his lap, a friend laid out in the back seat, wondering all the while if they could put it back on. Ears still ringing, but the screams of anguish that would echo forever. Like that buzzing you get when you're going deaf to a sound. Going deaf, but there it was anyway. And no digging could get it out.

They had patted his stomach and asked him how many sit-ups he could do. Was he going to college? Jeffery had wanted to lift his shirt and show them. Not his knotted muscles but the scars on top. The white fingers of flesh where the doctors had saved him. Look, his mom had the Purple Heart, the trophy of his wounds there over the mantel. Look. Because even she hadn't seen. No more playing in the yard with his shirt off. Nothing to see here.

It wasn't the landing gear that was open, Jeffery saw. This was a different plane. Something else nosed out of that hatch and dropped away, and he knew, with a horror that matched the last weeks of his life, he knew what they'd calculated.

It was a heavy bomb. It didn't wiggle, didn't succumb to the fickle air. There was no second-guessing its intent. A city in exchange for a continent. He remembered decisions like that. We'll give up this town if it means winning the war. Level the streets so there's no place to hide. A town for a country. Until there weren't no towns left.

Turbines screamed as the pilot pulled away, a jet arcing up while a bomb slid across the blue sky. It fell forever. Jeffery's body remained still, that monstrous side of him seeming to understand, to hear his thoughts. It was almost over.

When it disappeared behind the buildings, there was a silent pause, the fear of a dud, of nothing.

And then a flash of light shining through the streets and filling the sky, a billowing bubble of white rising up, a cascade of shattering glass and toppling steel.

Jeffery braced himself in that hollow head he'd been a prisoner in for too long. He watched the destruction roar faster than thought itself. He had but a moment, standing between towers of hope and despair in the shadow of his father's work—a moment to be thankful that the end was near, that the fire would come to take him and his brothers as well.

49 ❖ Michael Lane

Michael was going to hell. He could feel the inexorable flow downward, gravity and sin tugging on his heels, pulling him toward the center of the earth.

From the apartment to the streets, and now he was about to join the crush that flowed beneath them. He had crawled westward from his shithole neighborhood near the East River and into Tribeca. Neighborhoods that had been worlds apart now looked the same to him, all seen from pavement level. Cars lay scattered, abandoned in the middle of the street, doors left open, hazards blinking, obstacles it took forever to drag himself around. Newspapers tumbled across the pavement like flightless birds to attack his face. They spread themselves across the wrought iron gates and fences that protected walk-ups from the infected sidewalks. They gathered against the gutters in origami nests until a brave soul—the sports page or classifieds—tore off and flapped to freedom.

Shopping bags had better luck. Except for those caught on coils of razor wire, they fluttered up on the breeze like jellyfish pulsing through the air, torn handles hanging like tentacles and stingers.

Michael had pulled himself along for days. He couldn't remember why he was doing this, but couldn't seem to stop. It reminded him of a former life, getting up and doing things that made no sense, hating himself, hating his routine, the eternal disgust, and no ability to break free.

He used his palms to lift himself. Pushing down and then bending his elbows made him flop forward a few inches. There was hardly any pause before he did it again. Over and over. The flesh from both hands had been ripped away. Bone made clacking sounds on the pavement. Several of his fingers were bent back and pointed unnaturally toward the sky.

Groups of walkers passed him by now and then. They all grunted and groaned to some degree, weak sounds of agony from those dragging a broken leg or suffering a gaping wound. It was the accordion squeeze of organs like great bellows, wheezing and rattling as they chased down anyone still clinging and surviving, anyone with meat still worth taking.

A pregnant woman in a tattered green dress had made an especial racket. Her groans rose above the others, a noise among the inhuman sounds that stood out for being ... *human*. Michael had watched her as she passed him by, the back of her dress torn open, her underwear riding up, half of her ass hanging out, skinny everywhere except for that bulge of a belly.

He had lost contact with the woman after a block or so. She had drifted uptown on some scent Michael couldn't nose, moving faster with her waddling stagger than he could ever hope to on his belly. He had followed a different scent, one that pulled jostling masses down flights of stairs, into a station, nearer to hell with every painful pull and lunge forward.

And it wasn't his addiction taking him there. He didn't think any god would punish a man for being happy, for victimless crimes. No, he was on this inexorable crawl into the pits of hell for all the things his addiction made him forsake. It wasn't eating his mother, the smear of her trailing behind him for blocks and city blocks, leaking out his cuffs in oozing trickles . . . it was the way he'd cared for her all the years before.

Michael finally understood this as he reached those subway steps and began dragging himself down, another finger popping up to point at the heavens. He finally understood as he slid on his belly and the birds swooped down, as flames rushed down the streets, his torment and fiery hell not eternal at all.

50 ✣ Gloria

The darkness had a smell. It was the wet of rot, of cool air trapped and festering, the odor of mud, of standing water, accumulated waste, and damp fur. Piercing it all was the intoxicating scent of cooked flesh, a zombie perhaps who had fallen on the third rail back when it still had power. An impenetrable cluster of gnashing mouths worked on the remains of this accident in pure desperation. Hunger had driven those who'd stumbled underground to eat what on the surface would be less tempting. Gloria and the rest of the blind and groping column passed these pathetic souls by and followed the sounds of rats.

Their squeaking filled the dark subway tunnel. It reminded Gloria of birthday parties as a kid. It was the chirp of balloons rubbing together, short outbursts from tiny lungs, a jittery stampede beneath this much slower, plodding, and rotting one.

There were so many. Running over her feet, stepping on them, crushing some, them biting back with sharp and fearful teeth. Her blind legs marched forward, oblivious to the pain. Gloria's head simply remained full of her silent screams, her prayers, other repeated nonsense, loops of songs from a far-gone life, all roaring noiselessly in the hemispheres of her small mind as her feet carried her along.

She could hear the others walking with her, the squish of dozens of feet in the mud and garbage, their wheezing and rattling, their miserable pleas. This grotesque and invisible mass trudged downward into the darkness. Water dripped from overhead, occasionally striking her scalp. Every nerve was heightened by the pitch black. There were splashes ahead that warned her of the flood, and the scents that drew them in began to grow weak.

Gloria bumped into those who circled back. The gathering seemed to mix aimlessly in the darkness, trapped by the eddy of odors. She was one of the few who followed a slender tendril onward, into the flooded tunnel that sloped down and down.

Her feet hit the water, ankles covered, then her calves, knees, thighs—and still her dumb body forged ahead, following a scent and then just the memory of a scent. Rats swam alongside, their tiny claws pawing at her, scampering up her back and around her neck, riding her shoulders, little teeth sampling her rotting flesh.

Deeper. Splashes in the darkness as others waded in different directions. All confused, now. Just moving in order to move. A tunnel sloping ever downward, no train station in what felt like forever, and Gloria knew what part of the line she was on. This was the way. *Forward, forward*, she urged the man at the tiller. *Go.*

The water was freezing. It numbed all her hurts, soothed the craziness spreading in her brain. Even that organ would rot, she had discovered. It would go last, some part of this disease, some obsession that forsook everything but the memory of a life lived, gave up the body to save the ghost. But it was going, too. Memories and dreams fading, thoughts coming out of sequence. She was stuck in that morning haze where the nonsensical made sense for but a moment, just awake enough to realize things weren't clear.

Her shoulders sank beneath the waters. Rats clung to her face and tangled in her hair, little feet tearing at her lips and scratching on her teeth, higher and higher up their sinking raft, until she was fully under and they paddled away.

Gloria came up a while later with the slope. Below the East River, she suspected. The Blue Line was flooding. Or flooded on purpose. She rarely came this way. This was the train to Brooklyn and beyond. This was the tunnel that cut beneath the earth and popped up on the other side. The rats squealed with delight as they returned to dry land. They chased between her ruined feet and scampered over the dead tracks and the wet garbage. Foul water leaked out of Gloria's mouth, out of the hole in her cheek, and she didn't care. She was in the morning shower, nothing about the world yet making sense, not quite awake yet, not quite dead.

There was a soft breeze ahead. Rising. She bumped shoulders with another, a reminder that there were people in these bodies just like her. The darkness faded as distant daylight scattered down the tunnel. Black became gray became the barest of hoary gold. The smell of the living carried on the sinking air. Rats twittered, agitated, and ran forward, an army of scouts, the presagers of death and plague, the scavengers of rot and ruin.

Gloria was one of the horde to make it through. Bumping and jostling. They scampered over a wall of rubble, hands and knees, sharp rock, the roof of the tunnel bumping their heads, forcing them on their bellies, crawling and pulling toward the smell—and then an arc of bright light growing, approaching, until she could see the lurching bodies ahead of her, could make out familiar forms, soaked and rat-nicked and still moving.

The sunlight hit Gloria's skin as she emerged on the elevated platform, and it felt good. It would feel good until the smell of baking, decayed flesh returned. It would feel good until it didn't.

There was a train standing dead on the tracks ahead, stopped at a station. Nobody moving. An elevated rail a few stories above the rooftops. Gloria shuffled toward the train and the station, the smell of a place where people had lived rising up from the streets, driving her forward. Behind her, there was the rumble of jets, the silent whistle of swooping birds, the rise of new and strange suns to the west where suns should not rise at all, and a wound cauterized, but much too late. A wound sealed shut like a cancerous tumor, but not before it had spread to the liver, deep to the marrow, working its way at the very last to the most necessary organ of them all—

But that was for others to say.

Gloria smiled.

She staggered away from the city that held her dreams and contained her past, a hole in her cheek the size of an apple.

www.hughhowey.com

About the Author

Ten years after that horrible day, I returned with my wife to the place I was standing when the second plane hit. My heart goes out to all those across the globe who were affected by the events of that September morning. When I fly over New York now, I still see a gaping wound. I see her missing teeth. But she seems to be stitching together, much as we do. This book is about that her and my love for this one-time home.

Dedicated to The One Thousand.
You know who you are.